CLASH
HORROR

Beyond the Planet of the Vampires

Cover & Interior by Joel Amat Güell

ISBN 9781960988645 (paperback)

CLASH Books
Troy, NY
clashbooks.com

Distributed by Consortium.

First Edition: 2025

Printed in the United States of America.

 @clashbooks  @clashbooks  /clashbooks

Email: clashmediabooks@gmail.com

Clash Books
presents

Beyond the Planet of the Vampires

a novel by

Ulrich Baer

"Readers up for the challenge will be rewarded with plentiful idiosyncratic word play, poetic turns of phrase, and haunting images."

—*Publishers Weekly*

"Think Paul Celan and Buck Rogers meet up with the *Beowulf* poet in Nosferatu's castle where Dennis Cooper is watching the *Rocky Horror Picture Show* and you'll get some small sense of what goes down in Ulrich Baer's excellent new novel. Wondrous, strange, disturbing and sexy, *Beyond the Planet of the Vampires*, where 'words drill the void edges' and 'bonfires fuse borders,' is a riotous tour-de-force."

—Laird Hunt, author of *Zorrie*

"'If god is immanence, then we are already consecrated' Baer writes, in *Beyond the Planet of the Vampires*, but what forces lurk in that consecration. Cascades of language crash & thrum here, in fields of clover, in desert nights under streetlights, in distant cities, in 'god's profligate architecture,' in the hard planetary materia, crystals, storms, in eroticism & violence, a deeply seeking phenomenological consciousness whirls about, wielding words as mutable lumps in the surging, seething elemental forces. Grief wheels like this, & seeks like this, 'in inconsolable excess,' on a worlded planet where the mysterious other is encountered, fucked, punches, & fades back into the roiling mass of forms. 'The wound' he writes, 'thronged.' Here, he has given us a testament of, for, from, & inside of the thronging."

—Cody-Rose Clevidence, author of *Aux Arc Trypt Ich*

For Guy Hocquenghem and Lou Sullivan.

"We are not yet sound and we must avidly strive to be so"

—The Phaedo

"For the eyes of the mind, whereby it sees and observes things, are none other than proofs."

—Spinoza

"... the Other and I are the same person, the same dead foreign language."

—Gilles Deleuze

"the heretic has many possible positions…"

—Robert Glück

‹gue:

▲ Thousand Years Ago

It rises fuming from the catacombed, volcanic depths—the red swampland seethes and excresces sulphuric turmoil. In a collar of stars, that death-bound, the black sky confronting a vibrating orb, floating the mist.

Palpitant green fires.

We are armed with lasers in the backlands and slink through the permanight. I hide my back against the tourmaline cliff, beating my helmet against its jagged edge, lasergun clutched to my chest. And finger the trigger.

My brothers are dead beneath steel plates, herms for the forgotten—rescue missions. Condensing empty metallic strength, I go out across the carnelian sands. Stars slog inside the firmament, revolving without witnessing. The remaining cosmonauts crouch along the

vast open valley inside the mountains' pulse. They cr
pivoting around with their cocked sights. The orb begi
inside our minds, it eats away through the neural sheathe ward,
cataclysm. I brace my head with my gloved hands, unable t
the electric shrieking inside. Vortexing winds roil the sands, coalesce risen in foaming sheets, and dash out visibility.

I trip through. I trip through the buffeting granules, a bloodre
radiance. The landscapes consumed, and regurgitate.

Rapid cycling the eternadusk, I meet it on my knees. Unknown movement rustles and hisses through the receiver—standing above me, now. I throw back my head, dropping the burden laser it leaves an impact pit for a hundredyears, frozen ripples of contact promulgating-culminating formlessness.

Across immobilized time, he lowers his naked fingertips to my visor.

Inside his black eyes my dead crewmates bodies' are, are vanishing through, I see burning matrices erupting extended through pure unquantifiable spaces. Graphical pain. The scored field runs and runs—

With you, I have found the apeiron

And I will wait with you, through the mists

Beyond the Planet of the Vampires

Yr body lost in the luminosity of mine. Struggling air through the chambers in yr cheek, my fingers the wind catalyzed, mining the rusted mineral ore, leaves ticking pane glass. The veins worked through—a blurry scar on yr back. "Am I safe" you stop thrusting in and in and lower yourself, caving around my shoulderblades. Press aside my hair, "you're safe.
My cute boy."
The pentatonic scales, inventing the past, drill crescendos inside mine.
Fingers tongue and spit working it open, as a rotted bulb collapses in time. I don't want to remember

I'm looking for yr face in every mirror—

Here, Let Me Feed You Soup

I.

The moments continually destroy against themselves, ticking annihilated from sequence, and running down a pounding wall. It dims, unopening.

And we're in the basement mirror this grace to be
All of a mist. In the vampire's castle,

He is a correspondent, and I find it endearing that as he investigates his object, his love for it grows in proportion to his engagement with its micro-specificities, incrementally vibrating (like, throbbing out to be /seen), questions but he's not asking any—"Excuse me" he chimes back mimicking my accent—a cold hardening slashes across his mouth he's not going to tell me what happened.

"I know it must have hurt you." "Sad piece of shit" who is the addressee, now.

I am a running blur across the entry bells, the glass door hung and shattered back, this always restarts.

The movie star floats lazily in a gondola through the fog season, eating diamonds you know when they cheat, it's because his name is Compulsion. That you were drawn through a vector.

On fire, I'm tantruming the street is an injunction to laydown. Please hold me through the lacerating the wind exacts its funnel, forcing me to search for my face. When will we find You?

"Harold Washington gardens," he says "I'm looking for an heiress with a plan." I say, "When I was buried underground, I was afraid" (Because, God doesn't have any sonar? These Indelicate Fingers,) The moon supplants its song through the tensors that struggled your sentence to aphasia. An eclipse in thought, as Adorno looks for an intensive word inside an other word, where we can't hear, defaulting at the limit reified. And crumpling, recuperating recapitulating, drilling into a further wall. Beat your head, there.

I'm lost until I find the train tracks. The dead reckon it. Whispering, "please

I'm so hungry, now."

II.

I vibrate my finger inside you, you reach for your cock and begin stroking it a thousand putrid stars
facedown in the bed, ass sprawled up
Inside an inverse heart I gave /out

To make seed–spill a barren twisting field, squat gold studded the furnacing stalks, the sun cast shadows
They grind into husky gravel muttering, "fuck me." My fingers sparking dipped in penumbra, its orifice—vibrate my reflection.
Flowerhead wisps scatter-struck the rain falling, the clavicle surrenders: it's clouded!
Scales glissando, elapsing vertebrae tousled aureate dawn fingers slipped
behind a burning curtain, the Midwest structures—
The room holds its vowel, sucks the vacuum through yr mouth, objects disordered an edge-darkness blurs.

"My cute boy" destruction in a radiator, groaning. Muffled, its metal rasp clanged a prayer without intercession. Slow heat fumes. The mind flowers, the body language twins, reduplicated seething mirrors. Sheets. I'll drown now.

Because you're always / sprawled-up
In the melody, whinny for me
—sidle dimensions

Holy and improbable music

In order for a thought to be true, it must be in harmony with its object
He says
In order to be, it must possess the nature of being, which is infinite
He says—

I abandon my cuirass to the dirtfloor, in the dungeon of munificent vampires. The narcotic luster grinds inwards, words drill the void edges. Here, discordant thought spills riveted to that null behind it, swarming virulently—the cavity exceeds its tenets of recession—

I am holding a fire-scarred rose, ahead of my violent chest.

(My linen blouse, its crossing string loosened the white flesh
trembling with its purpleblack patterns don't resolve—the aching
parameters, memory his fingers, that the mortarworks

The granite mounted sconces rage with sedimental fire, casting green shadows, liquescent and pluriform.

The Vampire King sprawls across his technic throne, where wires seethe ramifying beneath goldplate plexiglass, peristaltically, circuit for his magnetic thought. For The Virgin, who lies on the marble operating table. Velvet curtains fringing the proscenium of his desire, fold hunger away. His legs are thrown over the armrest, as his face slumps-in. To a fist.

The virgin flinchquickens, clutching the white sheet at her throat, facing the darkchasmic ceiling. Her head sparks beneath the white crown of choleric stars.

I was not chosen to see this.

Having traveled for centuries through the bodypart trees, across the effluvial night disjecta.

Destroy me that I might remember
Nothing.

In the cabin.

I am punching a wall paint flecks run streaking, the drywall I am trying to find—
I punch it again, sick cracking bloodsmears what remains—a wall
Automatically I recoil, rubbing my wrist
An examining gesture that is blindstereotypy I am going to
Throw it again,
At the loosening—

Handcuffs that pulsate studded-in
The staggered ceiling, keeling stars
Its black maw—
The membranous galaxies peeled apart
In their gelatinous hurl

A tentacular expanse hilts the streaming
Thought
Fevers, tortured back
Down, in the body—

And oh, brutalized child, you are caught.
In deprivation, the in cantillating

Crystalline immobilization.

Earth, 3000 AD

I holster my laser and piecemeal like the sun, we begin recommencing darknesses. The planet involuting foundered, as I rushed all over the unworlded, the hologram spokelike apparitions. The oblique thing hollowed tones and I invaded my disaster-services. It pictures itself entirety in the sentences my mother uttered, collapsing-tiles strewed the floor. You're revifying in amber where the dragonfly screamed. An ancient syllabary strings from when, the one time my commander was telling me to play the song or I'll never stop hearing being its. The blast radiance widens, so I step pirouette the craterrim divulges its contours folded. A masterful deceit the time keepers embed-set the program right. That talking I quicksand and volts address themselves out. Am I revoicing here?

The white, dust permeates and a hail of thunder peels, we dragged through the beds I mounted a fire surges, before it knows it divides. He's music in another bed tumbling. I jar it, and wait. The director's hands broke-in to illegible timeframes, where you were sensing stars. Here, I'm in the onslaught, astral flocks disheveled wind, the courage meant I was its awestruck standstill. Please stitch my bones back into the aqueoussky vaults for me.

Delivering sermons.

I collapse one level another splits. It's impartial to the vanishing line, the thunderhead, crossing volcanic ductus. And the cinders delivered on yr birthday—the coasts' disastered, carry me out in improbable snow. I'm a child in a headlock, singing mutants. From the wastes of

A vine of infinite sadness slipped into the mouth of a storm

A vine of infinite sadness slipped into the mouth of a storm

"Eager for Death"

My thoughts were driven headlongdown an answer in infinity. Where I searched the treelines—God's profligate architecture, the mountains—
Shredded.

Massing on branches expanding harmonies, stars slowswarm the hilt celestial: the interstellar wind, dust studs coagulate—breeding paranoia. Slow flame crystallized green alluvial fans—in deeptime, the Heart clamps in thin jewel fingers. A charred corpse in the mausoleum, downing the night, I suckle between your legs, groaning languorous and lungful.

It spluttered, dreamily murmuring slivers shone—melting threads fallaway. The molten flood steps concentrated self: tramplehurt, en bas-relief, depths jumbled heart/beats lodged. Coeval roots towed draggling, a brined hand—

Don't think about the sadness of the hands.

The field, grain branches apart, twining thought petioles. Not-yr-own thought twinges. Nosing green tufts—summer wasted.

I am afraid that I am performing still
for an unnameable eye, in the vaults of being
I can't stop hearing / strange music—its
sourceless

Tear yourself out.

Fountain gurging, in the night you are. No one, at all.

He went back to his grave
"where he fell asleep again in the lord."
The subject of the disquisition

Terrible apparitions
—Magia Posthuma

"...for the notion is, that those who have been passive vampires in their lifetime, become active ones
after death..."

Tormented by,
Enveloped in whose burning coils

We go, vectors
In the direction of the unnamed
The deliberative ocean, waves unfolded
What surfaces to
Fully conceived / consumed by its own
Consciousness to itself

As if an oath
in unknown language

That tortures the body

Flaring nerved

And you with yr images
Are dead.

Darkcastle

He balances his body in the Darkcastle library, as I rip open a belt, and gushing out. Careening to cusp in yr struggleclosed eyelids. Pleasure grimace. Grope, densing opaque. I suck shadows through–
Yr body radiated. Electrical units of time, sparking atomic risen

It slaps against yr thigh, acrobatic meshwork selves contortion down my throat, vibrating. Tumbling through crevices, infrared concentric waves. Mysterious clarity

I need it I need it I need it
I

It splutterswhite and thickening against
Yr stomach curves—

I am watching you
From behind
The door of the future

And O, You are
Slashed

It converges, rolling Ball Lightning And I am an animalmaking destruction music

In the morning I surrender my head to the iconic vaults of the
library, its neoclassical murals of some white goddess of wisdom,
clicking microfiche I can't find
Yr face, now

With horror, in the Eddas between hurls of thunder,
stormdarknessing, I uncover there
You are—the Knarrdamaged child, who perished
A thousand years—

I see your blond hair streaming
Vanished beneath the glacial sink

Green eyes that focalize and find
Fire, tumulus you promise the peasants
volatilized in
The hillside, scored with

Cuadriculated suffering

He pushes his glasses back up the bridge of his And frowns.

You are making too much
noise, now

You won't exist.

And I am the same as anybody
In the dark

I press myself against his ass God doesn't care
Or hear me

Grand-sculptured

Porticos
I build my cock out of
dreamglue
And Nothing

Fragile shadow, tumbled glass light to iconostasis. Indecipherable, what inscribed clicking to the ideogram? (Feeling trying-to escape) Silence shadowwelling, hieroglyphic being, it turmoiled. Looking for: the signs-themselves. Confronting fluctuations, reinterpreted intensities. Gesticulate to yourself mouths—gaping catastrophe. Spilled filling intervals, you're unfixed? The intermittent names Itself. Hiatus, apparent suspension folds, unfolding mine—through the rattled sheathes of your body forest: combustion. My feelings gather blades. Take aim in designating unities—the sign circumscribes—blind ripples. We quake & succumb, intermittent clarity, the clouds smudge torn away—sole vestige in your lost arms.

When you're gone, I can edit you into something more beautiful, as time designs—

A snowstorm starts there,

Disarmonia—Prestabilita.

Yr false homology, the incipit. Wrought apodictic. Precessioning, its ends. Cuadriculated: gashing, we. Weft fire. Incommensurate replique, the rippled surfaces, I hallucinate their questions— His supposition of

Quantitatability, that precipitates the ideal thought talons—as the sea breaks its own path wayfinding / markers. Conceiving to itself—

And O, You are putrid still, in dormition.

The jolt when I run my fingers round yr heart. What mangled yr way in: to infinitude.

He envisions a black dog, the matrix's fiery wake. Thresholds among dimensions—just fog. Rake yr fingers, silver mist sequestered the self, in dreaming

Kant in his loneliness, Lacan says, eroticizing thought–

Shutters, the light abjuring from the room, where he fucks my asshole with his tongue, crystal waves. Hearing, Pluto descends, *As though / Something were rotting // Beneath all this / Softn.* The unseen holes. Smoky guitar riff, inhaling yr hair. The water tresses sinking. The reader resist, defers infection—promulgating along the vampire's archways—

Blackmetal tape

Sinewy waves, crystal facets matter to. Hallucinatory, this eulography to all my other deaths, e.g., dark rivulets swerve from the useful knife. Silence: yr cartography. The throat bends out-of-shape.

Cormorants in holy poses, formlessness spoke: wizening clack in the slackjawed night. Who is a hammer & pivot there. Like need

(Desire dies in / the sparkling armature of
Yr polymorphic dissemblances)

This is lucid power etching pentagrams in /to my bound chest—flowers embedded the field of my misfortune. Where a fascist ministers homosexual love, the lily anus smolders. Strungout in the powers of judgment, what you you were, discerned. And I defer decision—

So languished on the terraces—he says, “I am dynamite.” Defaulting on the train of mentally ill debris. Baby, we won’t find ourselves til after sinters.

And I am the furnace of my own desires I will have to die inside, a thousand times

As the world falls apart under Spinoza’s gaze mysticism.

I am reborn on the train, diamond hauled from the core I am. Alive, is that. What I am

I think the plane from Athens is leaving Mexico because my heart still lives there, enshrouded in lonely silverflame. Violent revelations of complicity in the stitch suffering that constellated farspeaking stars—

Shimmering guitar tones, I blanked inside. A song. In front of the iconic tourist attraction—caryatids obliviated its thought.

          And O
Yr fingers are burned
Fr touching
          And O

Orestes, Yr personality empties itself, to fate. Inaugurating some polis—purely exemplary men denominate, cutout fr the light

Having spent thousands of years building being enough to be received, be only yr fate.

The branch glitters, as fire edges frost with its penultimate—fire desires

You

Trace filigrees, snow flakes. The cells proliferated—seclusion. In the infinite substance, You needed me to be a man, rotting inside yr mirror—

It slides, and tumble outmined. In the excessive degeneracy of all you are.

Baby, come closer I wanna hear Yr epithalamium

He was a European, born in 19th C. Montevideo, and he says he wants to know
that hell is close to human beings

LIVE FOOTAGE: [REC] 12:34:55

A silver glimmer cutting and rounding the metallic dark
The skull burgeoning

He disappears inside the orb, burning the film strip
Focused on its touch—a red blotch

I lose all. sensation, I lose
All
sensation
I lose

I

I rip your pants downstruggled around yr gleaming ass,

and fuck you into the floor. *Fuck yes*, you groan in dirtied gravel undertones, hoarseness spent electrical-tape. I guide you into me by your hips, jag ridges. Crackling poppoppops, as I reenter it, staved-in.

I raise my arms like a penitent, and fuck you without holding yr emptying waist, rip yr knees away, and pound you into grimed woodboard, raking my hand through wavelets finding knots to tangle fingers to, I pull yr face towards me revealing the harsh neck swerves, throbbing veins. My other hand reaches its crossing the curving planes of you, to find yr jawbone, I twist yr face aside, in the hothouse mutant flower night. The abolisher glides through its rims, seeking, seeking

Kiss inside my mouth, while I

I hurl you onto yr back, and shove the useful knife between yr fingers—Carve the cipher numbers into my arm.

In a voice outside-speaking outsides, the sky is low hanging fog dissolution, the trees abolished in their secret—darktrancing silhouettes

Tinsel hammers. The sun cycles convulsively, flickering seasons. An eyeless stag is nailed in the wall, the hollow sockets searching light, the dead are disappearing to. In another & another dimension God works—You shake, as you drag the tip across my arm, revealing the burning integrals that buried them selves to flesh.

When it's done, I press my bleeding arm against yr mouth smears you suckle it. And I wrench you back by the hair to feed there, feed it back—

The grail of my mouth.

A fastmotion cormorant is blasted down by an air column.

I need it to resurface the planet submersing in my dreams—

Choke me until I forget my originary coordinates—the brittle points abstract in the desperation that searchedout
Oxygen

—Rotting lungs

Slender fingers print the suffering throat, trying to find the abbreviated sign, that abeyance alleviated in its suspension. Gesticulate that you are destruction's index, I pass imperceptible below the threshold vision, lucent.

This isn't going to work—all the angels are dead floating up the empyrean, the noumenon founded in mist.

I'm screaming now—Give me back my beating heart vanished through the rose quartz, fatality's harbinger, a structural cruelty slung around yr neck, the black wings coddled—

The seasons scabbed

In the Cinerea

After it ends, I crack
developed crazelines, my body crumples after it
ends, I start stroking an invisible cock—beating a hand against
another palmed
betweenmarbled thighs, nerves that blossompurpled from
the proliferate folds—I feel my proprioception flowing up right in
Phantasmatic Waves—
Spectral sensation, my body rushes with out

The Insane Excess that Love is

I can feel it, I can really

Eitherside of a diamond

Sensuous destruction

Intricating Absence

Shorts out
what abolished in
the mirror

Forestalled

Worlds, you are slumped there
Milky,
dribbling time

He knows how to take it
Throw his head, tilt it
Narrowed eyes—lips parted
Staring down to me
Moan

Bouncing his ass
Up&down   Against me
He makes me lose it

He makes me lose
My shit

Faceting the insane
sides
of a lucid crystal

Level 2

The room is hung with string membranes, vibrations knotted. They crackle with circulating light, passing between variegated, iridescent shades. Windowless and blueblack, the ceiling, the string membranes tossed through the floor. I can't find the staircases, now. Someone is speaking through a wall. Is there an elsewhere I throw myself downto. To feel a center. Gravitating.

I will always have. Stayed downhere, a long time.

Level 1

The plane is orange redfog without demarcated densities. Still, you run a flaming circumference, the surround revealed it only expounds, farther away. When an object is tossed, you cross it and race the circles, touching clairtangency. Time meaning only that you have to do it again.

The horizonless worlds

The electric possibilities of the referent field Collapsing—Allatonce

I am an instrument, please, play the chords right

In Veracruz, I lose my mind to the glittering spread of the night, rotating bodies rushed back by/ besides the wind: gyroscopic dawns, the sand shattered tawny braille. Hermeneutic scripts. We register our masks, and dissolved /resolve again—the wake of your board exhausting the night anguishes the pier stones, castigated by the rumbling waves, the sky echoes—repliques without intercession.

Revenant in foaming, despair in the howling-open bar roof / the stars chattered through the muzzy slogged dark. Slaking on the green branch, in the countryside, the fields watering horses, who stumbled alive to—constellations in yr mouth—Arcane concatenator. Who pulled the fixtures out, wobbling supernal fires, doused by rain/storms. The hurricanes that berthed you. Back to back to the sea—chambers hemorrhaging without remission.

Dynamite the dark, hungry for being with trembling hands

Touch me my outline, strum my reflexion extinguished

Ripples with out surfaces, I reach for you when I run out of music,
my singed fingers.

Destroy your wayback
to him.

My only trait is fatefulness itself.

Slowly they motioned with language as if suspendedin its gelatinous. Reverb errs. Look at yr Vampire King—a swampcolored brocade jacket. The sky grafts tints, vegetation gathered. "Voices are still" In the chrysalis. Beating.

The Planet of the Vampires

Iron rich soil
So germinate

Lurching elisions

Neuronal Temporary Being

The flames slow as if in prayer

Grey matter sparking in yr brain.

going to die on the ledge synapse of nothing. Pre-established disharmony, the sequencers transduce, adducing, that yr body was succumbing to my tongue, brittle bone forest and I think we could start running from the future, now. The vowels misshaped in the mouth, which ismothers. There is an instrumentality there, that rings the vaults, clangored. And we calcified I'm talking about the way in which once upon a moment of incandescent solitude I took long cars through the night, and we couldn't quiet, finding anything. My commander mutates and distorts, through rage, I can see his coming around the threshold. The door is the liminal space, we waited in, looking for our postures. Render a form which is upright and basically decent, with logic he asks, child have you supplied the faithful transcript of his deceit. My Father is a movie's ghost and he's grinding the lenses in a watchmaker's dream. Of the oceans, the oceans. The sand lagged, because the time enveloped, didn't fit. You were quickening with what's under: water, garbled music. My mother is a cottonmouth, and strike for me. Earth reticulates ends, joining with the chorus of nouns, that the possible field shapes never lose them.

The red in the clay is silence.

I will orbit his body a thousand times, until I lose my names in semantic satiation rituals he says, whose name is Totality? The satellite that defines the night you turned your headlights off, and accelerate the curves, the mountain carves its mouths to. The face's guttered. Barometrically, we're losing degrees, here, the cabin is a point in a place holder argumentation. So, I lookup. The electricity discharges in the ground, a circuit busts and I'm drunk on the wine from the coldstore of the funereal, the parlors present. That these biers will be defiled—is that yr name? Nerves begin: resonating. Threads, my thoughts pressed apart in goldmist simultaneities, the wasp beats and chirrs it's winging against the glasspane. That the fever held. I have to gather my things from the raw cabin—exposure symptoms. The brain incorporative uptakes its error margin, that scrambles noise, the mind resurrects. What? Numbers, chanting backwardswhen it's extreme enough infinity you'll throw yr clothes to the snow, packing the the creek edges, I ran in my boots carrying everything as the sky sloshed, tippling overforming gelatinous resistance—night, my steps direct lines to see a ghost of God, and Jesus Christ what did you do with her ashes? Disembogued: another word for, flowers. In the paludinal, the humid psalms.

The petal shed stamens miraculated, connection's arbitrary, the river ramifies by bearing, meander maps.

I feel through the darkness for my car, boots sucking mud from the watermirrory ellipticals, the tussocks pulled through. Ours, a coarse tufted, swarming world. The pupae oozed reversing the egg dies again & again, imagoes slipped their retainers—deposits in the accounting of an infinite substance, meaning you can't understand how farback it goes. The will flat lines and dilate in pupils, a thousand ghosts rushed through out.

Falling in love with the angel at the event horizon.

The moon passes behind cloud shatter, veiling, unveiling, I pass into my car

The oil refinery is regurgitating my dream suffering, that bladed wheat stalks, wispy, and flagging down

The breeze moves its mouth, duskmuscles, O the minerals deluged through, loudening fields
Molten, sparking rain—

Crystal lattices laddered harmonies, we diverge from trying to. Divulge something til inside/ out blurs, spooky tain. Touched its surface resonance. Multiplied hallways of the drouth, the lines course asymptotic searching. Looking-in, the wrong dark, with fingers. Hymn, gaining land subsides—its rocky porticos. Stand the moon, stilts, the thyrsus shows a void core, by crying. Whimpering canopies, like leaves looking for safe harbor. That need wandered, and inter/ruptured humus. Ragged, to go on flowerlets, that desire redeems chlorophyll. Systolic the mirror's vestigial, the body ruins.

Yr the salient bridge—dusty gardens, a light dazzled. Running vistas

In the nascent pluriform, cryogenic remains—icy exhaust

The smoking mirror, burnsoff slag, the truth starts blurring inbetween. Successive refinings
A radio memory, blaring in yr thoughthead, crowns.

That's when death lodged itself in my mind, a stream, the crystal facets. Tumbled out, notyet dry.

Tangling his fingers through the matrixial lines of my thought, he rips the whole reality structure

out, that I was so tenuously string to it. Irresolute presence, what are you? My lostcountenance, still humming ineffable. Untranslated music, senses were gradating valences, their shadows creep, so I know the scintillating passages of time. Trying to get awake. In the pod, infernal larvae froze in stasis

Kant is hallucinating Plato's rubric of infinite space. The body's still——still mechanizing spheres.

When he's gone, falling hallways of self-reflexive virtual reinterpretations. Is my interior re-presentation adequate to you? When he's gone—interiorized, a yawning abyssal the waves press apart on the nothing, that funded. Themselves.

Please locate me orchestrating through yr intervening glances, I sob into the voice recording, staticky grief. Sicker than. And he's silences. Subdued torrential transformations. Please come back, singing, I never knew we could be disastered hammers.

Destroy into me. In the ruminating memory inscribed, chronic systemic knots. The face—ashes, prehistoric fans. Filling in earth's lossless channels, silhouettes swim drenching. When the reasons why are uglier than. Truth

The celestial machines

II. When yr gone

It rips the moon out, chasmic howling downmined, all the land. A skeleton in yr closet, tinkling like shard glass fragments, sharpening their hungers. The body will usurp the mind.

The petroleum the river puddled, slipped greasy beading.

We live within a hollow beneath the edge atmosphere, and further in, the earth cataracts. Wind drives, carrying its likemineral to surface teething tension. That gritted it its bunching core. Liquid heart, ideal fire, the nickel mirrors snuffed.

You sunk in a pressurized room.

Alienated from the corrupted deluge, the planetary body welters: a massy configuration pitched through, and runoff sludge, still radiant.

The white painting the aluminum wall plates. The extragun in an alcove drifted (spastic), so splint it to yr thigh. Infrared waves caressed and pushing drove the body through. The angle of incidence, in reflection, the nebular pools. Thread thought, cognition.

Degradated—ditch margins. Verging spasming, and shifting beneath

The torrenting flood courses the world, wrapped around it's like snakes.

A receding corner shaped yr dread. Extensity.

Will you flood, comedown.

Beside the Acheron.

it winds until it falls downtogether. We cried propitiatory, across the stormbanks, down to the others in the lake. I have betrayed you, by my stainformed hand. The water purged, repudiating me.
Even transmutating across innumerable modalities

His attributes express existence in eternity

Nightmares sucking at the throat, allnights

Gone exogamous, is evil the desire to wed with the outside?

Involuntary transformation
,
    When You
Touch the sign

Compañero, yr in the gemmule pouch
—And I'm teething on the riverbank

El babeolento
del semen

o lágrimas—

What fails to
cross

Horizons—

Truth convulsing between yr legs—subside into you.

Trickling fluctuated, meaning spasms, under a maledicting constellate the senses altering anguish took to

The throat, incarnadine dripping, humiliation consummated

Galactic clusters—hallucinatorily extremities

I see a megacross, emerging and pulsing white candescence
to crown in
dark distances
Gone through / a veil you wearing, are

Grief is strobing inside yr body
until it goes out

And then you are a stranger.

You are spread. You are a disheveled chord, in yr neck.

Vibrate to me. Toss him in the bed, flip him in the within–surrounds of fire. Gaping, and my tongue goes—pink rotted bulb. Terrible stormeye.

Stroke it, if I if I let you, the sky conflagrates. Hazy darkening surges, the planes cut sunk through yr body, bifurcating running curves want to be. Choked gluts, the creekbed mouths. Wriggling pupae, embryonic dissolution, a pouch spills runny mist fecundity.

Like anointing new fathers, leather bites it in my torso.
An extrasensory bulging feeling behind, the bodyforms.

Convulsing seasons snowcollapse :: Opening/sky to—

The cabin. The mind is tornback stitches. Flex for it, & wait

Welt-born, blueblack, God is the infinite substance trashing in Yr arms. He bites it—when it's toomuch.

As lines divide towards infinity–their distance is becoming indeterminable. Glass /futures shattered projectiles, departing as doves exit through the bodywounds. Blindfolded summits. The horse you are, praying on knees

For that its substance is never corrupted

Images of yr shame confounding across the screen.

You need to submit to him, to make it stop. Strobing alarmlights.

Beckoned, the hard wrought emblems returning, as if one could.
Drink the image

What the orb took bundled, now nacreous, fed on vacuities. The
projector sputtered. A light beam fidgeted down the wall

Absorbing the hands that directed it

I am driving and driving back I have to get there before she's
Ashes. The cabbage patch kid dolls, from the closet
cutting room floor, the hospital
crying in a gas station bathroom
mirror, collapsing chains
Of reference

Allatonce

If God is immanence, then we are already consecrated
If God is immanence, then we are already consecrated
If God is immanence, then we are already consecrated

The wasted rain weaves its vibratory glissando anyway, crushing the leaves. The ground effaced, in the orangesilk fluorescence. A streetlight throbs, struggling on its guttural periodicity. Night, that the starfields drowned. The rust lines sinking. An electrical force–struck itself.

The ceiling was conditioned by infinity, it doesn't resolve into corners but continues asymptotically searching. For? Darknesses seep where the lines failed intersection, unknown, they are suffusing in through the unculminatable.

Virtual vertices—plasmic destructions route the liminal contagions, space doesn't and we never, feltdown from. The fuming antenna dark, sparking like a radio voice.

Come.

The wind in the room glows
Darker even than the rain's
Neonsplatter

Billow shimmering. Red throats tipping flower stems. The body is pronate

Cracking joints separate the insides pulped accelerant, water folds around. A bonedrill, the tooth sunk. Strands of seaplants, flowing towards—Flesh & fat, stuttering inflames. The water exhales—extinguishing them.

Floral dust scuzzed, resurfacing random lights. Yr brother's face undergoes the transformation of a million colored dots, hurled beneath the waterfall. Devoured mutating by botanical grievances, tumescing featurelessness for ever, until

In the vision he comes to, in a brightly lit room: as he wakes inside it, the auroral bodies of the aliens appear floating forward with slender, impossible fingers, raised toward his face.

On a covered wooden bridge in the Chiapas, this memory sharpens the light its name.

We will travel to the limestone chapels where water gelled time in music. A carousel loses its dimensions in any open field, paintchipped horses. Their horror white eyes.

Ruins of the cathedral on the hilltop, where the soldiers buried the Virgin, caving the town into extinction.

A bull flicks its tail, stiffens then the muscle undulates, releasing streaming shit into the stormyellowed grasses.

We step up the terraced rubble shelves, linger, and jump off, like puzzlemakers, the mosses dream their face across the heraldic carvings. The roof eonborne away, that god might make presence shafted-in supernatural luminosity. Glare, and the weed cracked. Rifted, the body, and fronds were dressing the floor. Smokeclotting, the aftermath

Beatdown.

Yr face like spectral shatter.

They are still deadlocked in the azimuth.

Torn hulk, the world over. Watching through the spaceship viewscreen, glitching now, electric vision teeming spirals towards the surface. Like fingertips where the pictorial could contact the textured thing, the cloudwhorls feltdown the mountains.

Their images are regurgitated across icy blankdepths, that plummeted behind clarity.

The blonde cosmonaut is ready to die for the telekinetic voice fording light years to be subsistence, here.
Cannot die—the alien song renders the distinction oblique.
Wholly cogitation.

An extraworldly-damaged finger bursts against the control panel, pulpgreen and shooting off the palm. Toward earth, a fallen star.

Rubble bright moments, in the blockspace slurred. We continued oscillating burned. Heaving, the meadowhead, when we crashed it. Green whispers, the day ribs crackingsky. In decipherable ruins

Go—toppling stars

Like yr behind a screen, and I could almost touch you

A place that doesn't exist in this world

The fractionators and the incredible luminescent swamp mystery in Xalapa

Curling beneath the barlights, baby you will lose yr fingers. For this love. He is singing in his veins. Muscleflinch. And the night hurled further away

Be whispering like chapels. By then, you lose your way in the hallway drunken dark, surfacing rooms of consciousness, the candle flickered then

Plunged in a blackout, he is leading you to the graveyard. By your hand, malformed stain. The mist coruscates, in the public fluorescence, tearing its fingers through the stones.

The moon convulsively disappears behind cloud shatter. The moon is sleeved, cuffing it reerupts. Terrible eye, soft hollows, a jarana is diminishing through the blocknight, distances slammed-in. A wet mound of earth, denuded by God of grassflowers, where he throws you down on your stomach, the clouds piled. The sharpening stars. Raging iridescent flares, this staved the sky.

A small orb swirls into being-manifest. An apparition, between rib cages, traveling uptowards the stillbeating heart, green neonlight thrums. Will You lift your torso on your arms, grinding the paludinal flesh, earth covets its damp. He falls on your back, ripping down the waist of your pants, revealing ass biting it in soft contours. Spreading—the orb is loudening—you clutch your hair, to maintain the symmetry of

He plants the knife to hilt in blackearth. Who is groaning? Defeated on knees

Scramble up jerking backwards, and throw him off. When he hits the sloshing bottom you mount and drive your fist into his jaw. The night ricochets in a thousand mirrors without ceasing or finding its original object. Self of illusion, the infinity of incredible mirrors, furnacing the light.

A creaking sheet of metal, above redpacked clay, is lifted out towards the moon. Inside its sediment smothered pit, a cosmonaut in a black leather spacesuit. Opens his eyes

The body is torn pieces, when we meet the floor

staybehind

Until you have introduced silence into his human mind.

The moon is also kneeling

You drink from its incinerating fountains

I find my demon, on earth. And I fuck him from behind. *Yes. Please*, he moans.

I am congealing in sticky pieces. So you can feel the full force of the climax, dismantling thru
Yr body, likerain

The event is destroyed-in. Its mouth evaporates, being its—

Billowing behind wind, hurled beneath the dark grove. Rearising.

Erect granite wrecks inside the mirror where I find You. Dream doesn't have memory: silver shadow. Tangling the heart cords, a geomagnetic storm, sparks begin with losing Yr contours

Repetition divides the thing inside a blazing assemblage. In the seven thundered vaults, heaven chambers. The lunar rays were clipping out at the edges of the seen, unknown clamor. Dragging the moon drowned. The night pitched over—an expression across the knees. Bodyspread, the lap beneath: burning palms. You won't remember, later, stinging tears crystallized an embryo pluriform, rage the universe dishevels through crying. Loosening clay ruts, flowering interior. Fathering storms. The sighs reverse—a particle wave. His body wrought clanging lineaments, fusing electricforce.

Confronting the hurricaning, the cold gunmetal vacuole radiates wildly. Where you rushed out

I have lost my wet heart, palpitating for it

Where is my—I don't
Need it

Disgorging spume. Wet ankles, tackling crustbound, inmists. The glimpse spangled, you can't understand its dream
//Light
Song from a disparate world—stoke obsessive flames

Pulsing dark—the time of the event fogs.

Running back through the graveyard, pulling your pants up to your waist fastening them barefoot gravel upends the desperate feet, the night slags. You are burning through the miasma. A small cross clinks againstknotted wrist bone, Jesus is wasting there crucified by nails. We cut our arms on the spiky grove, the branches switch breaking

The internal world is thrashing, the mind inscribed the image. Ticking its detonation curse, torn toward denouement. Until I find my face, smoldering like a nebular disc, eating it in flames. They lick through, and you run stumbling, the roots gnarred. A body is transformed into dry husk, moonbarking, and you plummet down the lost cliff face. Searching searching for your remains.

An artery in my shoulder is tappingout a code. You will learn to read it with yr teeth. Born barefaced, and whimpering, blood streaked ash. And fallaway, cloud detritus. We are moving towards the water I will follow to the estuary, the open ocean an electromagnetic storm. God's closed eyes.

Until the curling tips, salt stung, driving it in—make contact.
On earth—

This nothing porous between us.

Pumping the head, in the video stream—sloppy suction noises
Heavybreathing It's so
Big A naked torso aureate, downy bodyhair
You turn to the side, displaying the soft curves of your waist into
Ass spread toward the camera, unveiling
A black butt plug, a finger lazily draws itself
Down to the

And you crouch, resting your body on the calves
Cut off the video
With invisible fingers

"To surmount it by willing it—

Mysterious need
Deforming the structure

A consummate expression
Rarifying singularities
Race to—

You are voluminous, spacedark expanding—an infernal gaseous cloud, ropy fibers of elemental beginning. So surround, and flash teeming into me. I uncover my solitude in your mirror, infections.

Codetermining differentials the world is starting to. Fallapart: Potentiality's face.

Rearing, a solar storm crowds the horizon—crowning its division defines—when you were a faculty conditioned to it. The particles sputtered, and jangle a glittering aurora. Witness its emergence, in the palimpsest interiorized, the sky shivered and contracted, now dilating gone.

My boyface

::Yrs.

Haunted doubles—that interior obstacle gives it its fundamental meaning. In resistance, labyrinth of interferences, the trees cast noisy shadows

The ceaseless action from without. There is no out /side we're already in

I can take the tone of my voice apart? Softboy scoria
The supernal vaults discharged—
Falling bodies flame accruing weight, upon impact, penetrate successive layers

I am marching down the spaceship hall, the metal baydoor grinds, opening. Automata are screaming in my dreams. Behind the threshold, that beyond the subterranean lust surfaced, it invited particularities to proliferate. In creasing visions, ideal lines wrapped throughon—Earth. Desiccation's flowerhead.

I float towards you like darkdarkdark, botanical membranes, the dry wind unfolded across the dunes, sunlight throbs the air you are a slender boy in a dry canyon, herding cattle, ahead of youryour sweatglistered forehead. The searing sign, fascination. Repulsion, when gazes make contact. I wrap yr throat in my fingers, and lift you off the ground. Suffocating in my palm, the life—breath extinguishes. Exhausted from strife, the principles you are thrash and flail, trying to meldagain. It won't work.

You have to die so that I can occupy the hollow softfolds of your mind.

Your brown eyes are burning, then smotherover with relief. As the oblivion holds us, it comes for you. Frantic, energetic spasms cross your body, cresting waves of expenditure. Your feet jerk to still into their rest of time. I drop your corpse into the sand. Heavythud.

My high leather spacesuit collar cuts in my jaw. Thoughtlessly, my arm caresses across my diaphragm, a devouring infinity. You course like sleep there, we have come to. We have to come to smoking halos, the orb ordained its eternal spread.

Interplanetary biological war.
Its movements of energy, surfacing the globe.

You cannot control its ends exceed you.

Jerking off in bed, doom metal pounding, boys who pretend to be straight to become gayagain on video mount eachother in successive rhythms. Pull the cock out and look, awe struck, then shoving it back in, then. Hazy parlors of low fidelity visions. They celebrate their ejection, into the unknown configurements, the dimensions accelerate, cutting through.

My genitals, my muscle tissues atrophy within my protective suit. There is no design, but maintenance. The undulate air, heat spent. In a blackout zone of the desert, we begin our stiffwalking towards.

The highways, I have to get to my mother's body.
Before it's gone.

In the desert, saltcrystals spikecoalesced across yr bluing lips.

In the text, You and I, reader, arrive at a wall of flame—pushed and pulled—but evercrowding the shadows out, come closer—

Then, there is nothing.

And you just weren't, and now you aren't again.

It's okay
It's okay
It's okay

and, then?

The orb is singing—*Do not be*
afraid

You just weren't, and now you
aren't, again.

PART 2

Not Human, Almost Mind

for men the desire for beauty is always the desire for death

Can Violence Be Reciprocating

I position you on all fours, bracing your legs, "good boy." Pulling you by the hips backagainst me

In the aftermath, on our backs, stiff across the bed, I will ask you a series of questions. When I hesitate you'll demand that I

Why not justsmother me down Why not just strangle me to—
In an evacuatedspace
"Hammerhead," you say, before I can answer how did you
Because you love to beat your head against me.

When I was drunk on my 20th birthday, I fell down bashing my
head against the floor a visionless automaton stumbled into the
bathtub they found me
Crouched over the dribbling water, repetitively, beating my head
against the metal faucet

I knew intuitively, then and now, that I was trying to knock
something out

Abyss of annihilation

Interval without substance, the mortal edge.

That extinguished the lisp-narrowing slash

Brittle darkness at the neck. Chain of tiny nicks, the night-runneled.
Furrowed raw puncture the dark echo.
Defining silence

Raveling :noise—

Spilling light, low smoke charred. Still aglow—sliding ripples

He cast back inside the blackflecked striations trailing gauzy night. Flaming knotted wrist bone, where we were modulating Interference Patterns. Slow as a failing heart, heatstains. Prising the light, strung precordial. Leaksweeping pearled

The heart/beat spasms, slowfaltering its diastole. Cloud-colored. Crinkling inside, its face, hairblurred. The tendrils wetfloating. Then—come in from the fog

Imperious, sashaying shoulders—a gesture of human weakness.

Drenched in fucking grandeur.

Dimmed trees, ashy morninglight, insubstantial depths muzzed sky. Holes eyes dug, vising forth. Skin. Gusty breath—

At the farend, darkswarming. Words couple then, debrided. Flesh from sinew, unmeshed. The radio drooling in the recess. Strokes concupiscence—that this gesture may never be abolished

Perceptual lace the deerhead entranced—spontaneous particular unknowns

The synthesis of all men—molecules arriving a threshold, fogcast back. Grinding

Flexing repression, the body drones hammered

Does the same event occur again and again and

Touching dusk.

Metaphysical language,

we look at her. Then look away.

Darkfolding place

Opening always, holes fracturing. Lightningstitched shapeless heaping border/lines.

Throbbing twilight, through a rayed hole, frail smoke blankets, neutralized. We hazed in returning clouds——

Yr body, fuzzed nacreous featurelessness. The filters wrapped it in. Messed-up and streaked numinous. Hunching around you–yourself. Coagulate column of light. An instantaneous composition, bronze flickering corroded. Energy cloud envelope. Aura you touch through—

And we were
Wayfarers—Inured to

What in my arms

Inscribe it in my flesh. Leave me numbered, scored tinder. Rent-rendered be. Divided—the moon smudgesout

Root stems bunching valleyed, the nape fizzed. The cliffs out tufted grass

Immutable object, fallenthrough—a plane,

You—stripped vestige.

Shackled by the orb. Pluriform mutant nrg's. Yr imprimatur—enter mesh bucolic. The body inter/raptured, his mouth O, sucks hollow

Pummeled & drawn on /spasms. Are you still? Heaving. What quality informs you, imprints you with its fire. The ideal subsumed roots profiles/ pushingout. Dull aches, it diminishes the horizon foreshadows—

The felt-heard down, sweat of the absolute trickles. Invented to pulsation, it's fueling tumescent vertigo.

Ambergris crumbled, later, in the falselight, whose miniature cut apices diminishing. Through its increase, the cathedral spired. A vacuole—twin language: grasslets snaked. Quiet searching words concatenated, teeming, saturated by porous Structuration, our filamentalselves. Streaming hands the ultraviolet caresses /surfaced

Holding that night inside you.

I am always surprised when you don't appear. From the fog. Even when I had imagined I wasn't hoping anymore. At the lacunar edge, this is the worst thing

Our Boy of the Evening has taken the orb's drugs he feelshimself disassembled by the night, smearing his shoulders

Sick with its coursing and curdling, I wanderstumbling from. Nocturnal to nocturnal vale, in an undefinable space—as the night pounds on the door. Fever

Chills, in the flux I can feel my heart complexing, slightlymuscle chirr—under the rib. Cage wind howling sounded, the part that wills it. To stop
—Is already obsolete

Heldin
The moltenfumy thrall—

Then you steptransformed

into Eternity. Staircases the moon dissembled by branches, glut tangled and overturn turmoil in the bodies disposed—pharmacological capital.

On the grey beach the flagrating sky the clouds maulraking deeptrenches as the sun sets. Flames in the material world. Outpast the border bursting its frame rapidity, and slownesses congealing, murky waves stilled towards the crest. Frozen composition.

Guttural sewage regurgitating the storm laden, infernal culvert's eye

Prehistoric, the vampire squid mounts your board tentacles caressed climbing knotting towards you. Immemorial spikes, eyeless mind.

In the dark, you dismount to, strange lights in the sky. The children with binoculars further up the grass clotted dunes, searching like god, the inexpressive face bricked horizon

Thought, like it's a visitor from another world. The oblong, smooth iridescent metal, the airship ferried

Cocaine from the south to the secret airstrip in the forest, met by military forces, under Duarte's gaze eminence, a dynastic malediction.

But, for a few brief moments the ineffable haze auratics of desire crown the sky with glorioles
A supernumerary and extratelluric finger, across intergalactic fathoms

Pointing towards—

Godlets, gurging in the mouth of streams.

A rigorous haunting commingled with the blood possess my molecules.

Vectors of need twisting seizured, the nightmares until you. Resurface. Every level like a metal detector for truth, the substratum fuming crushed gold. Finding only error, you submerse again—

Ooze unrelenting, what you are. Expands nets, the river trawlers divining your secret. Nature is public design. In the thematic sex motel, God of a thousand mirrors shattering starfusillade upon a closed door.

Drink, and be exhaust. Drive power through the whiskey bottle. A maternal ghostblaze fidgeting in the chora.

As a commercial of AMLO's infamous jet seeps into the television screen, mounting the far wall—

Down the twin aisles, a smiling commercial guide, a raised hand

Indexical signs hovered over the gas station neonlights.

Exit right in an opaque room, murkinesses'. Twisting fingers thru blond hair rusted—ultra fluorescence refrigerated white metal shelves, and you were tossed there. Figuration smoldered. The person at the counter stares through your face. 20 liters of gas. Please. Your gesture went on to the shadows, the night slungout stars it ricochets rejoining the origin, people crowd, flanking you, the sparse truckers like snaking tussocks. Finally, looking only down, the attendant takes the crumpled bill. You exit rapidly through the bodies that won't part for you, trailing the nebulous. White duststorm, and time erasing—

Topping a nightmare. As if forever.

Slow drizzle coagulates at the feet. Tread through gelling durative. The ministrations of the priest, fledgling gestures culminate an empty profusion, signifiance. Untwist the cap, and shove the nozzle through the gap. Viscous iridescence pools. Clinamen aggregate in systrophe, mustering forms. That Anything falls. And space dimensionless, so you were picking up local coordinates. Afraid of the mirror, speculation where You can't find, scowling towards bathroom tiles, grit caulked, and grey streams, the dirt follows. The music separates again and again and.

Ugly German countryside, marsh symphony. You dash vectored, on a reconnaisaance mission for the castle beside the sea. Stalled beside a windeaten herm, the men in black suits swarmed yr car, crawling across the roof and hands shattered inside though the windshield. Beating, bursting, greenblood. Deserted yr vehicle beneath a tree, overhanging the riverbank its velvet fronds, like bat wings. Laceworked, gesturing the wind's vocable. Having witnessed the burn splattered village, lay your body down in the hay mounds, a barn shed to the peripheries. They disgregated, now floating, lost wheat stalks.

Unbutton the doublet with clumsy fingers, struggle sapped. A woman will appear with a knife. Take it.

Converging points of reference. There will be more, later? After barns, gorge fallen. Drawn up on a platform, sentences casting mold reflection, suggestive of yielding. On the next page, it's still raining.

Country train tracks, alone
The gulfsin harmony.

The granite bathed in the mystery fog, a fiery ship casting ghostfingers towards the bouldered pier—

In the dark stuttered night, his fist flexes and finds my face. Crystal tatters, my head crashes against cobblestone. Clutching the weeping orifice, I rise up unsure, head hunched behind an arm swinging wild. In the auroral folds of his sailor uniform, his thighs like pianola script music, churning in the cloud envelope. Insolent irony, lifting my chin.

I crouchdown and pull a knife from my boot. God is a texture from which you will never come unlaced.

He comes again, dripping magma. Sulfuric breath, gusty irradiant. Slow capped waves undulate from. His bodyforms, tombs. The musclesmolder, we aren't released. Won't be. Estranged from self, when his thigh locks mine. Route him, a blow to the shoulder. Cigarette butt splayed between lips it falls castigated to the footed abyss, we wander sinking. Smirk and yr knuckles make contacts with my cheekbone, the bridge of. My nose, musical sobbing red panicles. Stringy runners, the mist folds—I fall in a black out. The treasure chest of yr body fuming above a syncope, what the black night pulses closed. Later. Oily tangles of darkness, pressing the form downed.

Vast angel of yr grief—the greensilt sun.

The unconventional pronunciation of yr sentiments, galvanizing oblique worlds

Vivid smiling, psychedelic hyperchromatism expanding oscillations you sundered from swampland effervescence. Pink cloud, horror lurching cypresses. In the New Jersey dark, and you were shuddering beneath my hand.

Electrical signs clipped out at the rims yr body holds: noisy desire, searching circuits. Slipping signals flicker. & Who will read you

Painfully white, glimmer clashing—the meaningful gaze spirals the body obsessive, mounting mine, fingers finding every

Reorganizing-scrambled with need, the twin star engulfed tipping into mine——by the hips
Sunk

He who has poisoned my mind, in every act: a solar disappearance

Violets clumped in yr body I try—plucking its contours don't twang.
Pounding with blue irises, where yr eyes go. When you close them

the room shorts, returns again. Irremediable elision, flagrating soft
lightning, my tongue finds

it why—yr eyelids

"towards the pleasure of his voice"

cascading tumult, but you are all gentling

feeling the blood chirr inside yr cock, inside my mouth
vaulted

my chaotic knightlike chastity—ridges you

"my cute boy"
the glowing rings of yr mouth

Resonate together rigidification, came—disentangled from my brothers, blindfolded.

To be entered and demasted, pitchpoled—transposing selves, shimmer dipped encrusting skins

Landlocked there—slow disintegration sparkled.

Taking feral being, dissolve it in littleboy tears, under my hand. Close yr eyes and I will lead you behind fiery nets—

Kidnapped on horseback, bluehaunted flesh

Tear-away the fog—virility, above yr element: fumy spurting

&I am plotting out yr bodystar charts, I will cull and cultivate the points drawn flowers spray cusping

Varying degrees of organization, crystal waves bloom, my tongue sentencing sounds overflow the cupping, intimate division

Dance floor strobe light, hallucinatory hallway, grope yr way towards the opaque. Sink up, freeing shadows from the red, puckered world

Rutilant arrow, reticent in its sheath dawn

Sounding, the bodies—bridges—lapsed.

He combs the dark apart.

The grass blades lisping through his fingers, thick white flashes. A strange aurora gilds the canopy, casting its Halloween light swishes enshadowed ground. Startled, he hesitates, sucking breathback through teeth, heel drawn back like a bow. A man is whispering through—he will cull you from this dim depthlessness, he will harden you against the barkscrape.

He's runstumbling now, catching on barb vine and kicking up the dirt clodded. Go down on yr knees. Leaves snake around yr mouth, mulch embedded. The stars sinkhole crushed sky. Blueblack velvet darkening bruise worlds. His hand finds yr clavicle looses uptowards the chin. Blue eyes ignite, then lids fallover. Searching for so long

Dewsobbing filters through branchlets. Trying to find. Backyard, a fencepost— "Lost, lost" he murmurs to the unknown, fingertips. Feral speech. The wind shaves muddled light. In (cosmic) submission, the fog breaks, unveiling the cosmonautical body. A towering lifeindeath, antinomies twisted. Shudder when it breaches gelatinous blackening, throbbing the air pounds back, tightening space buckles its diagram. Finding fingers, the clotted bulb, and shreds denuded

His glacial truth, drumming inside yr darkembattled mind.

Softer than water, touch through him. Translucing flesh

The orb is vibrating and growing halos
Rushout
Halating

Tell him what you want
blend yr thoughts
into Mine

Only yr shadow
& mirror
, ember

Wrappedin folds
Bathed in—the mystery
Corollary to the sea

Slowdance with him, into the mist, the waves softflung
coruscations

He breaks the 40 in the street and holds the jagged edge at the taxi driver's
face you are going onto
lose yr mind
fr this this is
a loss from which You
will never recover

Anthemion, Anthema

Yr finials—an ekphora, rosettes—its apsidal period

Flare into voice, vicariously

Languid tunnels, yr hollow metonym. The moon sent the clouds on—

"yes emptying"

Endthroated, sonar hands enwreathing /writhe. The sea in shards, threshold—equivocating "An alien vector" sopping treasure. Ravaged the river's wristing

Ulcer of light

Garlanded, hemorrhaging world. &You, inflorate

the crater isn't   *blanks enough*

The grave mound, heaped embers the river won't rake. & the film etching sheets, its lightmare seethes.

Vow vowels, the heart drains valves pulsatile. Suspension tanks

Fontanelle fountains, you gurge from—paring the wound. Fixtureless fault/line, crowded cells gold dawnmelt. Bold stud, don't struggle. Dissipating voice. Sink his countenance doubles, insidious speculant. Lush, stormsudden. Extreme indeterminacy riddled, the bodyholes. Feversick. Smearing the nightglitter—aching orator, the blood doctor will come in the next scene—

Who is shining in the mist

An identification behind relationality.

Riding the cadaverous horse into the desert.

& I will lead you behind. Curtains of fire–waiting for the coup, thistles deathblown. The only reality to which you can lay claim, is contained within yr voice—

Revoking yr world in silence

Denuded of songspeech, the image unfixed.

My mother's voice in my head, long arms tugged toward. Nowhere, now awake. Almost

Abreact

Encased by sound waves, the funereal grail of my body reaching
towards—Yr mouth

Days of inscribing, the words that finally break/through
circling days' bruises, and tearing cascades until—
They crash in

"It hurts to be this close to you. I'm so scared

transpiring away—phosphoresce,
recast falling
in
& out of
time

what the system
withheld

Thickening & thickening

Darkshining. Radiant hairfalls—the soft white of yr stomach. Intangible rites, in yr mouth—mudbricked slang. The stalk infloresced. Slightlythrobbing spread. Goldblack exhaust—the bedrock.

"The forceful master of an imaginary virginity"

Fuming in the synthesizer Mexico dark, nerves tongues blood, systems of. Filtration—the long slow hands of the water have been reaching, trying-to, find you. Here.

I traveled for it, so long. His statuesque boredom. Nacreous fulminous casket—

"Even against the winds of heaven"

Suffering male indifference, in the spooky bar, melancholic twinging. Fog billow slow unwrapping meaning, scum-driven.

Rumpled permeating torsos. Brutality. Almost unreal-stark mirrors, without object.

The hardset base, plucked forward. Shadow boxer, losing yr match with outside, in the thrall fusing Yr mother's body. On the table Wolf/boy transformed. Guard—lay yr vigil down.

Struggle-dragging yr wings. Topped a lake inferno, we coalesce, umbrous cuts.

But I would be a flower glade beneath you, mutating lasting only its season. Raucous, caliginous ports—

Tenebrous, being held. The body blurred in myth. Glorioles. Architectonic constructions riving, integrated circuits, virtual & missing—

Fallaway incoherence, from chaos, emanating drawn circles, unleashing fluctuates

Reborn—discordance, a tidal flux snared:

Instantaneous actualization

You trace grooves thru—which the river will carry away. In the dust, the dreambeaches glued. O, cleave to me, pith arcadia suckled.

To be an object of pleasure, I will render You in/ to. Pieces— O, the desublimation of water.

Slide yr fingers down the glass, *He is walking through the rooms*, tousled branchlets

Nectar //Ichor—moonstains

Smudging—lightning bolts. Greenclouds. What can't be encapsulated by the image—overpours, I drink there.

Tear away this profusion.

"He was a careless, laughing sod Who had no fear of man or God."

Gold encircled, working its way into the dream—lips parted. Spasm, almost exploding—tucked blossoming. The Undersides of Petals, Voicespread, likeshadow

Darkshining bulb. Pressed hands on lovingly, imprisoned. Wanting to present a provocative gentleness through the chest. Strange ambiguous, being-flinch mutation's. A marbled thigh. Striate, I'll spoil you—greydust mantles.

& You dismantled there, floating imperceptibly

Go, unknown—

Go.

Bluish veins, almost an image. Unadorned dusky. Dazed, the trophynight. A vineghost stifled Him-on-the-table. Crushed flower. Gnaw-aching transmuted structure. Unearthing. Never awake again—stone pages. Thought myself thatsound, teaching you to pronounce my name, with fingertips. Thrum, willing to surrender. Burst morphing like tropical plants—molecular corollaries

Trembling being/nonbeing, eyes bore thru—antigravitating. Twitching muscle ligaturefabric, anaerobic night. Oxygen clamped downfisted. Unconscious insides writhing, outsides. Proffered my past, hands cupping crystal shards to. Desire's face: fluctuate. How the dead watch us: eyes slipping over

Surfacesurfacesurface

He wavered on a threshold, stepping tremulous, the onrush behind him—howling chasm the night branches—

Im pers onal wit ness.

When my mother dies I crash inside a series of sexual nightmares, be. Coming a sadist. In the bad dreams, New England forest. Orifices bitdown tissue. Murder creating identity—mutual between us. Specular doubles—

Re-presentation itself, breathing there.

Rimming what tangled ceremony—Yr grave cerements. Sterile emblem. I carve yr body::Mine

Reloading, at the site of yr grave reentrance, splendor rotting.

Divulged

What?

We were wet on the floor, in Mississippi.

That You were, drums out it doesn't echo. Soft gauze streaks, and yr body made up bandages. For carolers at the funeral of yr dissent. He's an avant gardener and I'm looking after the image fields, the quarrying. You took yr horse and set it free. Blue mouths, the mist spoke portals, and I erased through. Race through. It's cinder, and wasted the coasts, as you swan neck curves a gentle blond and mares disdain the castoff legacy. Yr a wintering—I am trying to write my mother down from heaven.

Mississippi Mississippi Mississippi mudslide song

Snorting snow clouds buffeted the banks you are. Shreds out to sea, white quivering the moon didn't slake. It gashes. And sashay yr drunk on the embers, the fire is crying. With the farspeaking star lights. Blood on the canyons, the bow curves and an interval breaks there. I found you combed apart in duration, I am trying to see through screens. My translucent hand

I need to live in the depths of the sea beside Jesus. He walks the night shade in. This is not an injunction It's an imperative that you know what hand holds you
out

The fields run ragged—

The red in the clay is blood and memory chains. Hologram filters. I am in the church—rapture me light. God done castigated he done cast you downed, in the firmament is ladders walked up

Axis mundi, a snake coils the cosmic egg cracks. Its filaments go on without me. And you are sitting in the mist reading love poems, it was you.

Who disengendered light the gold blurs, the bars banded on the radio receiver. The curtain drags tints in flames, I have no memory. You are passing behind a rainbow—I am shedding skins. The water moans eating in them

And that he gave his only life for this

Metonym, the pulse line it isn't Enough

On the EKG, keep speaking to me. Count yr fingertips blessed by the waterfall crush. I just say the same words over and over again, trying not to describe you

Depicted—gone out

The streetlight changes colors obscure neon stasis

I don't love nobody at all now Pls Forgive yourself, pls

Make yourself up in the bathroom mirror, lipstick blots. A purse is endless misery's. The cache that held you, fogheld back. I want to see you with clarity. The undertones surceasing, these new techniques. Spasming on the seismic detectors. You spoke like splints, and a mountain cragged there. So now you're speaking birds. The lemon tree and it undresses its hands. Amber caught yr eye flecks wizening cast-off skins. The marshland tumbles and we will revisit it in another, and another act—

I have not yet written—please keep summoning me

All that catches in the light is the ghost imprint of his body. That punched out holes in the matrixial space. The borderline skirmishes, all night I am so alone to be tired. I write but my hands quicksand, melting forms trust thru. I wanted the light to be softening but I was too many voices in my own head. Diphthong and divot on the cross, I have no new words now. Only hesitation and this accrues debris—I can't walk through the star slag. It eviscerated yr song to.

How do I feel myself down a rope, the knots are on fire. He says not to talk to the dead but I know, I know hell's screaming in there. The charnel churns through the groundworks. You turn into an impression it suffocates did I ask for this—hands. Nothing in the world is. Music culminates in this moment, and the next—gone away rupturing everywhere, you thought you found yourself out. I need to be less noise now. Quiesce and flare like solar discs, coming alive.

I wanna be fixed like god fixes angels I wanna be fixed like you fix a dog

How much disaster can you incorporate in one body

Be quick
Be lithe

Backland sermons

on the black porch

where I learned of your death, again
& again & again &again &
Jesus God, help us
with this subvocal, substructure
breaking the mouth—

wound/damaged air
do I deserve my suffering is that
a real question
I punch my fist thru
the night

& ricochet

Stratified, underground—this forgetting kinematics, submitted to.

Transformations—the black irises that time felt, falldown from it/
self

Terrible mutating panoplies

Crying in front of the triumvirate   in here: cathedral,
triangles strigillating gold/lines, the fiery. Revelation of

                    He makes love to me with his handswhispering

How much electricity is flowing in a given area, in a unit of time
trace it with your fingers. A real enumeration, membranes mold-
fusing tear-away

          In the shadows of the infernal phallic signifier,
The gold dust sunk in—bodies were atmospherics

And the solar wound, defining—

Syntax unlimited words leap amorphous. Cover one nostril with a finger, becoming. Inhaling. And throw yr head back-dilating irises, pulsing the increments of. Time, simple stages, for Aeschylus

& the metallized, shimmer crossing the proscenium arches, infrared reaching hands pushed through. Yr diaphragm

The navel: center, its cord tugs sinking, resistance. My tongue.

Bruno Ganz is watching from the rafters. Like Mary, a pieta these appendages we shed for love, polyphonic chrysalises. A brutality, in the blood I need its noisy in/coherence

Where God is coming for you, through the reality screens—

Slung across the bed, my crotch packed brightening. Submerged meaning Yours in the dream: duskmuscles of yr mouth.

The crystal enclosures, You sunk Me /thru the rotating black Self luminescent diamonds. Disintegrating, the exhaustion fr i d e a l space, the vision enhanced from sharing its parallax with

circulating haecceities—

Shoring up, the night ruins

The beautifulevil twinks twist alive, in the frame
in curled fires, from the waist up, naked
smirk towards the camera, between rapid cuts of cock
Stills. Gelling vignettes, smoke meth then, the smoke reverses back
in the body, back to the pipe, unformed even—

Glittered torsowet

"You are going to lose yr teeth for this
love"

Its images strobe–

A cock a
pentagram pentagram pentagram ram's head cock cock
cock Smoke cock a Pentagram cock cock leather Bondage a
pentagram Smoke Bondage a cock pentagram pentagram cock
cock cock Smoke a pentagram dribbles cock cock cock, cock
Smoke
being

Submission

—Freedom,

Or

I want you to fund the wrecking pulse of my body

Unmarked helicopters—
sensuous destruction

Tooled wind.

flaming driven mineral, creases evocable rivulets circuit. Itinerant, vocables rooted ash, shadows weighted anchors unfold—muscles in/ter. Wedge, quivering still, rockburied reflexion, the mirror slips its sheer surface, in worked fires. Syntactic slake, snagging fastens it serial. In/ductive propositions

The heart of the mirror—bunching threads.
Puddled, squarebright. The sky is braying—longfractures quasared stoking cardiac, the light washedthru. Looking for his heat signature. Rinsing through the visor, fascia eroded

Cosmic dereliction
I felt less real there

Under knife, the intestines spilling radial. Electrically scorched dangling fleshribbons. Body pinned pendant, systolic. Waiting for its release, light pushes in, weeping in continuous relation

Existence pertains to it? Islandlike. Limestone the statuary face bathing the living-dead. Over the energy drinking—something else

Dreamed in the land/slide, photovoltaic. Torn fog, seafounder

Moonchords, the specular words, unveiling soil the glimpse tipped in

My commandant

and you are forests, Orestes transformed
circles convulsive the citadels hounded across
waves—the red drunkback sea
slender ankles—dipped birdwet
bit bedrock sunk
metalsound

clamor, yr element—growing wings

Desmotes, I must /shall have been chained-at This—Desolate seacliff
Veins that rake the earth body down

On the stone slab, omphalos, my mother is a psalmodic ghost

Please keep praying for me, Apollo. Hermes, wind yr instep with mine, the caduceus

Hushed, the interlocutor, gone
radio static

Greek cosmonaut weakkneed in the dimensionless. The only action
left is to rush to, star chattering shrapnel, tinfoil teeth
In the muthos, mouth, the cosmic /kismet
streams—

Transgressive Modes of Address

A world scientifically and coherently established. Caught in the feelings-nexus, You rattle and alert me to
Are you alive?
Allow his elements to pass through you—occasional flashes. Understanding, new formations complexing reacted touchingoff. Bedrock—

Stratified feelings—Historico-social figurehead, ramming through the shadows

Seeking seeking to erase—the worldtotal vowel. It collapsed in side Yr Mouth

Reaching for yr nomination, in the verses.

Intercalary ipseity.

Boy of the twilight wonders, secure yr head for passage into the defamiliarizing worlds—Sleeping pages, No memory. The body wreckage, only this formlessness

Fell on yr sword :: ejaculate benedictions. Ganging, split. Silver rind, the grottosong hunted for

The low flaming red sun.

Once you twist away from one name, you can slip a thousand—lost to the field of reference
Brace yourself against a tree, to enter his room, gone past the threshold now—slit the painting open, and slipcrawling inside where he will you will will

Have to die—in the redlight rush proximities, an intergalactic storm, casting down the trees. Rip off yr shirt on yr knees, open the belt and plunge the knife becoming a line, like a splash of blood. The insane horizon—

Brambles, chivalric wind

"Faithful to the cause" you're serving. And die—

Cogitative terrain, where he formed you, cultivating stems. From forgetting noise, the backdrops.

Wires through the uncontrollable channels, blurry figure in the densing mist. The stars were taking hold of

Never be Dogmatism's

Burning Gestural Grammar

Fossilized, subterrestrial. Yr ossification procedures, progressively, the body unmanned.

The Law as aesthetic. Soteriology—menacing proportions, drift spastic. Timestilled by the fog investing it, plunged into. Divested of purpose, fall pierced—head reeling in the mystery mist. The disposition of the dark trees, chambering. Or chapeling. Collapse of the dream ensnaring, brought into contact with horrors—degradation, subdued thunder came glittering across the water. Sensing discordant meanings approaching, the river crashing—broken waves. Melancholy, an enormous wilderness transfigured You.

Metamorphosis—enveloping strata. Igniting the spirit of enterprise, its plunder became vocation and destiny. Immobilized in purchases, land speculation. Disappearing into the mines into the factories

Las Casas proffers testimony

Ideological aesthetics miraculating-cathecting commodities as emblems, signals of luxurious rightness. The desert devoured: In the briars, in the briars

Stonemouth—the soil is alive. An index of Uruguayan suffering, Maldoror wrote backwards. Fractured mountain communities. A priest with a vision in Guadalajara—

And that's when I was struckdown by the thunderbolt of death
What did it feel like, to be gone so long

Like crawling on the surface of the sun, through mud.

When he breaks the glass, when he rushes, when he jumps the kid from behind, when he is pure, fuming rage, against the totalities we divined I know him as myself, sign radiant outside my body

Rotten star—

When my mother dies, I start tracing the constellation of suffering across the globe, twist flinching points. And you are caught in the scintillating electrical pharmaconets, the dream blued. Bow yr head, and submit

When my mother died, the furies descended upon my body like studs riveted from the sky. Drink fire for a hundred years. Net-like garment, taxiing planes

Geometric Light, Bending Undone

Propositions, capable of referring to others, neither true nor false, enveloping significations immediately understood, identical to their manifestation.

In speech, I heard you, I heard you, as soon as you said—

The acoustic image jangled
-relapsed—its vertices

The vector: a stormtorn boy, from the south—knight in the sheaves, the fire started to /written into uncertainty. Flinch chimerical florets, behind the mountainteeming devastations. Life crossing you yr eyes:: flowers pearlesced—

Ghostplant. The grave rims. Ratiocination of jouissance frequency crescendos desiring the death-in-formation. Recharge there, ramified—

Postures, still life? Productive modes of suspension in fluxing: representationality tableaus, that you might be trappedin. Its specular dimensions overflow the image where it drinks. Dramatic personae "highly formed."

ledgesin the sea, the sea is streaks
we are the anger we waited in, awaiting our
selves our
selves

When he tells me about the taxi driver fight,

he has to sing it on the jarana. I am so ashamed of my infirm mind, its metallic cruelty radiating wildly like a beacon. Quirking untranslatable vibrations, shattered against what surfaces And the night clattered in around us, as the black surf, so broken down. Think for a hundred years.

His hand finds my throat, then loses it again.

The pier sand flares gold under streetlamps, running, and shadows punctuate the boulders. What you traced into that spatial interim, won't return. A lizard scrambles across neon graffiti

Years later, I will do anything to prevent myself from tossing myself into the Aegean Sea, pink eternal abysses—no, Orestes, keep the narrative straight— In the rockphantom grottoes. These control rituals, performances in the dark for some towering Poseidon, we meet when he locks his legs around my torso. Flaring irresistible light to my eyes, intertidal beams gushed. When he was a littleboy, he would flick his mother's eyelashes. To fall asleep, so stubby fingertips brush mine. Flickering quiescence This isn't the world I wanted or invested in. Everything harshing and unreal. Alien quicksand—

"But if you're a boy, I can't love you," he whispers. And fall asleep inside this rotten cavity, I carve.
From

Outpast the docks, and the orb is shaking!

"What I really like about him is that I lose myself in him."

revolting in the mirror rims—

That the mind's excess, kiss his torso, the taste spread—

Move against the mirror, you could founder—with one shoulder heave.

Damp bodies step down from the frescos light wounded, colored shards fell.

Unmoored evil matelot, floating in the dusty silences, hunting out yr ghost in the corridor shafts of red light. Renunciations from on horseback occasions, people flow into, distorted as though lifting a heavy fog. Crying in the Mannerist painting

As though I'd wanted you ever

My mind in the stormdark antechamber, unwinding thread from the damask eventline. Alien affect cloud, garlands a stony eyed voyeur. Annunciation angel, frozen gestus, the repulsed world regathers there billows—fragments from beyond the grave.

Cocked his head. What heaven I pertain to, pertains to me.

Undressed sepulchres, I want you to tell me who I am

With a divining rod, a tuning fork against yr temple, sound waves caressed spread taking possession. The steeple of yr body between my penitent palms.

Sharking spout the obelisk, a vaporized bobbin unspooling, spooling its again—turbulent silences. Unbearable entrancements, when you touchdown.

This deepset grave of my heart, stigma where I buried myself. A glacial silhouette you carved out of air.

In the nightmare cabin, ineptitude I claw my way inside yr diaphragm, searching for the secret pouch, you spilled—softly trembling blossoms: eyes that open in surprise, a pallid halo re-meeting you across the deepends—

Yr body's vanishing in the alphabet of mine, carnal matrix where we were sonorous-fondling in figurants. Terrible crypttexts, palmswept, and abandoned.

Beneath the stadium lights of yr bedroom, the body is doubtful urgency

Yr on the passerelle again

The lapsus are deeply felt–falldownagain

He touched against the bolster—rough ashlar.

Wanting to disentangle—becoming enveloped, anyway.

Your asshole finds my finger rubbing at the opening, the rough folds, slowly swallowing it wet tissues shuddering, yr voice registers the incipient release from. And so I vault, to catch it in my mouth, as your body cataracts around. This. What I fail to drink spreadstains taking possession of yr pallid stomach. I lick

Wanting to see how long you need my finger inside you. Guzzling its pulse, like eternity sleeps

Little volts animating my face, when you're gone, coursing with cruelty—poison sliding noxious now, an infinity of stars. Delicate wrinkle filigree crossing

Torso Heart Anus Calves forgotten Feet, Stomach surging—a lost vapor of the virtual, tranced remembrance. Desperate aperture—dredging agitation. I am a sensitive boy cord fulminating conductions, the grave cast bewilderment at the revelation of

My heart hurts me with its pining, branches obsessive—you whimpermuffled and flexed—gone.

Littleboy fingers finding the chain around my neck, to tug gently, realizing me solidity.

Signification, never homogenous, denotation never grounded circuits—swirling incomplete—

You disidentify from the cock, between
your legs
—crushed beneath the stomach
open palm against the bed
surrender

when it's in
when it's in
when it's in

side stars you fall apart
concatenating thronging Nothing

flocks broke
the sky

everywhere you were, you feltlike doom

ugly thorn caught mutations

nonpulsed time, by its nature
that it fail—

involuting
and exitless

He steps through effervescent

He steps through, metamorpho-lacerated
He steps through

Sepals sobbing

And why does he need to rush the blackout, what sentiments does he holding, holdback? Feeling the thrall of the avalanching unknown precipice—

Carried away in the dissolution, grace abounding: visions searing eyelids "little warm shocks" the pollen of yr touch

In athracite/reason, the body turned to stone/myth

Sacrificed on top of the wave crests—drinking abjection

Burgeoning, flourishing, unveiling and re-veiling itself, lace nets, I am never finished, re-entrenched in justifications, some one proposed—

Two figures silhouetted in the window, a single bed—nunlike casket,
the arms akimbo. And glistening, they conjoin with My Shadow

Acts I undertake to feel, the glittery swirls re:memory brackets
Don't. Struggle, breaching come alive within me.

You sound like crushing stained glass and water purls, there is nothing else in my body
but penumbras aching and the lost weft of a singular thought

Do you know what musical noise yr made from, in the darkinfinitude

Can I kick and break loose from all the horror, what I am. Sleep in the grove, seen behind the eyes—

The mystery uncovered. Needing to top it, and brutally
Jesus Christ, is that why we're already finished?

Pantocrator, My God, My God. I guess, I
I guess so

Eat shit in the thermonuclear waves, forces of absolution you played in the syndeton, plectrum plucked electrum fire—wants its conjugate—jagged in forms, coalesce sharpening.

Blue dust vessel inflamed, yr lungs—endlessly blackening, as death throbs over taking the cadence that ripped yr mouth—crystal shards.

I strap my dick on and slowmotion flip him over in bed, locating the epicenter of your body you'll drown now

Coarse waves, throbbed denoting that space is with out matrix, its rubric toppled in the folds quivering a reticent hush, the gardens slowflicker frame apparitions of

To-rot

The petals bursting forth. And you are thrown down, bottoming the well of my body

Write another note and I'll
tear it

ha ha ha ha
ha ha ha ha!

brittle ghosts
releasing smoky portents—

"Wrap your blanket round me"

To be an outlaw, burn all yr shit down
And run.

Slow preparations of the gesture, naked trans in Zipolite, you are what you are this noise, aberrant to what sociality.

Depassement from the whole field—

Across time's congealing darkstatic
I am wading towards You

Dimensions razed, when yr eyes lockmine
generators
Reborn, in the threshing that wrecked out

Infernal boy machines—The inscriptions of his metallic voice,

Yr cock is shared between us. You my uncanny ghost
&mirror referent—

He found—birdhaunted, rockhollows

Carved a diamond from-the-gangue merging facets, presented for subsequent penetration. Without exchange. Sheltered him by the wall's mathematical hardness

Dark beauty crystal, stinking knees slip tangled gorehole, entwining rapture

Ray to infinity, escaping horses through your body

Tried to reach beyond absorption, the gaze that held you, backwards

Seismic rifts, almost ourselves, erected wrecks in
Evil

Strident fantasy machines

In a leather harness twist yr shoulders, to heaveopen

—a body before you. On the dancefloor forensic scene, letting strobing flames engulf the case files, jerk into stillness. The wall mirrors were forges. Almost finding the tenuous withheld, breath in my mouth, stagger backwards when the pulse can't be. Located in the onrush, interlocutory triangulations, when so many gazes converge: mine. Destroy yr maps

&Tessellate, a boy who was all weeping crystal fractures. When my hand corrects your body slipped the orbit—a refulgent torso. & deviation's. Melt inside my mouth. Iridescent flesh, soft pockets where you embezzled yr secret

It cutsout. In the next scene, I come around a corner drenched in mist, the walking trailing lags a film strip repeats. Flickers. The lost word for yr armature, lay it on the table of night you seduced him across. Guilty erotic murmurs, the synthesizer pounds the shadows downcrowded. I lift yr face, jawing delanguaged in soft palms, the stigmata shonethrough. Flickerflickers. As you tug off my shirt, you

caress the field of arrow holes littering the surface, tiny hemorrhaging points. The thresholds cross themselves. Nonontological particles you wrested out inbetween—muffle yr face in my chest drawn flaming down the central axis, where something is stirring awake at the apex, thrumming a visionless eye. Stuck, the reel jammed clicking its cartridge empty, now torn
Shake the hair away, chiming wisps. The glitter resurfaces this world—

Touching grass tips, confusing music. As he sinks, the sloping valleys towards—

The desert crystal, sloshing limpid seaglitter. An industrial site—at the climax
Kill yr lover. At night, you were looking for a cell to holdin
The eviscerated organ meat, groaning, sliding out of yr chest

This stench prevailing, mortality's harbinger
The branches are holding the fog—

This crime is the point of yr departure will you hesitate on the verges, laconic bloodsmeared saint. To prevent him from crawling, bind him to the night's cords. Rendering predatory hands

Insolent smile, bearing the littleteeth.

Flickflicker.

Homophonous contaminants, sinuous infernal doubles.

Unnatural bondage. Mutatis mutandis iterable, it repeats thatself multiplicate, and dividing internally, these cutting edges—hyperbolic identities, indeterminately oscillating. Proceeding with a hand cupped over my eyes, deciphering etiologies—vitiated beneath the examining hand. Its causal chains ruptured

The gesture discovers you / his: libido sciendi, a study that suspends or sets aside praxis in a going on towards exhaustion. Of its objects

Solved solvents then loosened, when dissolving, more and more engendered by the blades sensual, constructed when you grazed me. A heterogeneity shivering transformations implicated, involved in the scene you were trying to interpret—

The look mingled with incomprehension's horror

He is breathing through me

Inframundo wind chamber–jagged, multidimensional
Hallucinogenic word poison, signification's effluvia the stars
flooded the body—frail bonfires.

Nightly concretions.

Malleability in torsion contorted yr facegrimace pleasure moan, the mist transmuted into a fist crushing transfigured thus existence. In circles

& we will be carried away—

Time exploding

Disjunctive architectures relinquished, this barrier's between us

When identity can't be present in—itself-invisible thread that endures.

At the center, grief catalyzes—ever renewed in its power. Loss' magnetism that disorganized space—lines deformed across proliferate parallels, flexible loci, shifting and contingent, the self mustered from the tree mist densities. Then, cast in to the night

Flinching particles, the desperate homograph agglutinating histories. A grapheme etched some vibratory weave, where you sundered yourself from. Embodied differentiation principles.

Flaming knots, the blood flooded hands, twilight glows on. The night shimmer interlaced with yr flesh and sinew—wild daffodils—shallows overflowed and vanquished them. Disappeared broken lights, loosening the cuffs. Idiosyncratic mouths, doubling inarticulacy

A winterfire sun /shaft spoke of—the holy thorn in my thigh, ex-branches contingent mutations, architect—sound. Wanting to be, in the littlest grottopulse of yr thoughts still

Green.

Stars of blood in the mist where yr hand, already, no longer belongs to you—transparent and erect, ejected string jets. The overgrown sumps, woods and thickets, blur yr face. Muzzy and partial wholes, the porous border/lines. Heavenly bodies flumed slow, beside the ramparts, stripping the billows—turn and vanish again. Languageless assassin.

Ruminating dreams, the drainage filters—collect detritus, you soften catalysts wanting to. Unravel—that death might pass through you, outdistanced the fog season, hushing tectonic plates subduct and now, resurgences.

Came de-scripted from his touch. Yr lover—the heavenly blueblack bodies could float there—clover heterogeneities, the moss beds velvet / downy tussocks unrooted, the sign he carved Affects—

Eating the night diamonds of the air collocated, the mountain chains. Sublunary nature—crushingout

The non-coincident unsamed there, for hours at a time, the curtains of the cabin, ignition battered by the wind run glittering from another world.

Sexed identity seams. And amble blossoms

Crying over the shackles the moon pours fire and sashays through pane glass, ending the night the syntagmatic trammels—

Touch's residua fomenting, in the profile, a face darkmasted. Grafted within /to its overturn

The fuckplateaus, I came apart in my father's whisper, trailing fringes, the fray tattering silver gauze of the sunken face. Countenance it in division's last sacrosanct gesture.
Yr mutant thoughts—

The extraterrestrial objects etiolated under—intensive study.

An inter/ruptured message across the space fathoms the radio signature, gravity wells. Creation/Destruction mythos. The transmigration of—

And the static is burbling, accepting dissolution's hold, now. In the galactice armature, fiery astral nodes, cosmic dust clouds drawing cusped

Where presences superheated—

Multiplicate series—on its knees sheered, algebraic concatenatory. Hyperventilating, the body incantatory. Only wrote the proems. I buried my language under the tree, cerebral mirrors lacerated. Anemones rotted when—yr arms divided the fog.

The films variegated me, time justfractured. The sumptuous nettle ditches vectors destined for formaldehyde. Meadowed a decomposing head, the crinkling evening star deluged the yard. Death acred there the bleeding fantasmatic buck—

grass tufts
purple yr hair for me,
grief, rippling wave locks
the depth of midnight
tree canopies harshing densing
the dream carving

adagio
blossoms tumbled,

the grass sings as you scramble it
thorny branches clung to
the velvet haze
heap of night, mechanically seeking
the center, the self in execution
on the table
progressively, becoming unhinged
manifestly, detached from bone
violence punctuated and held the silence–
tortured clavicle
tumult, the river rockflowers
deposited beneath the flaming Wall
of Death, flint struck–rattling its error message
vaporized the dimensions
you were holding down
hemorrhaging through the mind

Bits of signal, tasseled. A house for hulling spume, you begin with stuttering, storming foliage susurrated psychosis

Inexact portraiture triassic ferns gilded—

Watching my fingers sink your waist. Grabbing, that anchored the You-on-top-of-Me, it feels so good I have to look away, as if from horror I bet you
Love it, eschatologically,

In this next scene, I I finally jump from the ferry into the Aegean Sea, I'm Hart Crane's phantasm and I never want to be foundout—
Tell this empty image what I am, with fingers

A cosmonaut plummeting downdrowning through the hyperpinked waves

Downdrumming, the pulsed.

I hope you're dreaming about my lengthening-mutated trans [ ]. Huge and red, enduring dread in the dream fugitive flora, yr body running streaks—Gaze into my eyes, the heart chambers vectors clickingempty, like a gun cartridge. Sniper in the grass, wreck me.

Floated in the feelings cloud, electrical dungeon. Riven the earth's veins you mine film. Mineral tissues will cover the fire tatters of sleepdrenched hypnagogia, unwinding in the cathedraled shadows. Did you hear the birds—nuclear wind.

Reduplicative, metastatic cells.

The slowrevolution of arcs. That bludgeoned the window you were trying to see thru orchestrating silences crescendo.

The talisman of yr neck, cities collapse salt sewn, its loops tightening—unbandaged time, bottoming the basin. Hush.

Diabolically breeding receptors of the anal orifice, origin gulping—
Wear away, hearing it, ever.

Localized sensations scrambling coherence. Wanting intoxication,
my fingers spreading yr lips
blooddrunk and gasping at the nadir, the anchoring the deadweight
plumbed lines, only tangent to myself
Again & again &

Were you just / satiating formulae—

Characteristically disorient the garrotte, soft compacts with violence. Obeisance, before the ax—feudal livery, decomposing fumes, alarming—alerted the villagers to the site, fresh turf overturned—

An outre, and make it yrs, abbreviated in exclusive acts. Carnal dramaturge, descend yr teeth inside me.

Resonant intoxications imperiled the losing altitude. Ivory pillars—
the in/sides screaming

Craggy silhouette jetted cordilleras—undefiled worlds vibrating in yr arms, overspilling jeweldom.

Ectopic, in volution, the plane only always simultaneous to its unraveling destratified, floating affective clouds,

Torquing, yr bodygiven harmonic functions, crossed too many

spaces—

Formal resemblances corresponding, silently, dissolutions made to echo, inarticulate faces. Sonic emissions—incredible fibers. Drawing you back to what

Petrified curls.

"they can't execute me every day"

Internalized my gesture, in my mind, seductive points dilated. The ray of the body that found: yr eyes plummeted-to the pit of a stomach. The sky membranes ruffled that need–festered dripping candle wax, lymph of yr thought seeped still hair tussled glorioles

Pierced him—delicate tremors, nostrils flared I
Turned my face away

And I would follow him down into the darkshaft

The confession concealed by the buckle, yr waist slumped exalted repose, its element and chemical sign. Mossing the pelvic floor, myself no longer

Almost imperceptible particles—

The gravity of yr stare—afraid to look now. Cast back in the glance. & the body dissipated—

And I, the same, was reft. Come of another nature calling you back with the supernumerary, invisible hands, the cruel smirk of masks crouching inside power's oblique recesses.

"And besides, hell, I've got all that jewelry!"

Shadows searching for a vertex—

He is bound with the threads of evening

Shaking against the wall, caress his thigh, the ass that finds it apex in the glacial center node, wrinkled and earthquaking, the somnolent glance, needing to be, rush—
Sucking the nipple like a storm daggered fawn, the chest tuft, where flowers drown the ocotillo branch aching thorny reaching

Brush the sky vault
To be—spreadopen, lanced
Thunderstorm prey, rolling the desert boom
Serial vibrations—

Hyperbolic geometry disheveling through yr chest. When gaze meets its intersection, cutting lines razored—pass betweendimensional

Becoming man, beneath your ass, the soft swivel curves then—

Surging in my mouth, the sheltered head, stormdarkened

The pier light, outpast the juridical inscriptions of this world

Jutting archipelago. His monstrous body, the flames rent, in the infernal conscriptions, find blood in the grail of my mouth.

The soul transformed across its tinsel trimmings, trammel the unknown, and drink there.

Exhausted interpretations of the mystery, drawn by the hardness of his metallic voice
& cuffs, he doesn't struggle.

Fleur for me: a stiffening braggadocio.

Secreted dissipations, the milking stars flood—the sentinels were setting fires on the plane—

The antehermeneutical I, unsealed Yr lips, freeing time signatures—this play of limits. Yr body all seayearning, castigated against the firmament, instincts transforming disseminate dripping Blending masc/femme indiscernible lineaments, in a nexus the matrix set.

With the generosity of this gestus, finally, undoing yr self-limitations—on the table of eroticnight.

Jesus at the crux disconnected illusions, snapping wires on the floor—

"Countless causes that never enter experience"

He went across to him.
I sd, He wentout across to him.

Diedaway

Composing a veil around you, in the poems, the line is still screaming.

Trickling stalactite loosened the dream clamped down by the atlas torsos, that penetrated the lung hollows. Appearing under my eyelids, discontinuous destitution

The lake of sand disarticulated, singsong eulogies, to the guardian of the law.

Desire is not illness she says, moaning through the hospital bars masses of color swelled, muted light—that light, sound fell backwards

But I am so imperious on the horsewhere he buries his face in my back, arms flung around my torso, "it's so sexy when you lead" We are going to drown in the crystal, when we arrive we will be deepset—in the grave of evil, the slammedup horizon that finally belies no secret depth, or interior.

Electroshock reality, people searching desperately for biodeterministic gender, in my face

The horse's heavytread across the dunes, quicksanded, and the aching torsion of yr thought like branches do you want me to still them.

Flies that settled some secret putrescence

Cariño, we'll drown now

His violence made me feel more real

Object of rage against my fingers

Insolent, the haughtiness of his desire

Float denatured, polymorphous

Eroticism directed out at the whole world, as fluidic tissues enveloping it

Sex, and never unitary

"I folded myself into his body"

Poles of positive or negative infinity

He went out across to him.

"You're going to have to come apart here in my arms there's nothing else."

Field Epopees

Apparitions of tenderness
The dead just looked away—

Scraps tattered

Scrapmetal, scrap dirges dismantled

Felldemolished, in the hour's violets.

Mutually coalesce—wanting to drown in the sea

Pitted, the body hallucinating yr body on top of mine, kneeling then castaway—salt vortexes. Rimed with ulcerations, I hushed them in/ down yr skin.

Operatives mining bright spooled minerals leaching. The vascular cavity. Thrum diastolic in my arms.

Coronal gagging flesh.

In the collarbonehold on—

Euphemistic gravemist palinodes

Garlanded you—diaphanous worlds, tipping flower stems. Catching flecked the light cuts the line. Screaming in the index of desire

Torsion came fumbled apart from My Brothers. Axial, now pivot disassembled—

II. Vow Vowels
Engraving light, sighs inflorated diadems rondelay—
stars stars

Capacitating the shelves. Sleep in the sulphur trail mist. Notches the vertebrae you form
toppled ladders, recessive ascents

Rib bone courage pulsed the stalk, still ventricular—
Inexorable zeros zeros—combed galactic dust

Interstellar wind—the muscleline. Smallestshadowy liminal, you couldn't crossback—alarm lights.
His cloak brought the stars whirling. To cataclysm

Trailing nets, dragged the knife across—squeaking droplets. Crystal, raindripping

Paso doble, match yr instep with mine.

—When he catches you in his arms, drink from the fumy chalices of my mouths, the sky chambers. The stars were breaking out in lacerations, the mirror hurricaning our faces duplicitous redoublings, refurnacing. Ion beyond being rayed thru /coruscated the fog, the body tanks.

Sleeping hothouses. Curling panicles ablaze, felt yr glass hands searching.

Flushed—mercurial. Found you in that sink, bottoming bedrock

When the blood leaves yr body behind it.

An inhuman gape, flexed yr torso. I'll lick it given contours, a vector to

Smokestains the cabin walls. Gaudy, like tinsel, instruments of torture.

Lacking configurant, deliquesce be /reaching my arms. Yr itinerary involuted fists, when I clamped down—surrounds of fire

Heat rippled, evening you jut stoodout against a field, I buried my lovers to.

The orb will reentrance the minds, its metallic shimmer cutting the round chamber, the skull peace. In hyperpieces vibrational, belowground.

Resurrection mythos, behind a cloud the unknowing : graveturf rumbled and brokethru

With a charred hand

& the fingers were *trembling,* Earth ciphers—

In the oubliette, the chandelier uncurls its smokedirge,

stillveining flowers shook & stiffening, the unctuous curves treaded a continuation, pastdimensional—

Limpid skin. Gone
were yr irises.

Violent stems battering catalyzing the unelemental infraworld gales—

On yr knees now

Transcategorical submissions

When I grazed you yrs yr
Body transluced

Fulminations sapped hands, the wound
thronged.

He takes me back into the hollow recesses, and he knocks me around

Seeking the puissance that flooded
the veins castigated

Steadied myself against a wall, locating the membranes that space
stuttered-divulges itself in naming
silhouettes undressed
—I crowdedback into myself
Cheek swollen
Swipe at the blood trailing the lip
Blueblack gorges

I try for a hit to make
Contact
As the apocalyptic dawn grooves the bathroom, glass panes
Ruddy and pernicious, he throws my head into the linoleum sink
This will cup me until

I find the knife in the backpocket

of my jeans

I throw my palm over
Yr mouth, paschal mysteries
were frothing
Reanimative speech, diglossal
the tongue you split
teething on a choke
utterance
As my pocketknife
finds and transcends
the arterial injunction, you lived
—you'll fold now

Limping back to my car
in the desert, undulant light
—parking lot desuetude unfolded the heat's hands
white spume that made my lips
mine, from ganging chancefalling
materials—

A 19 year old boy is tied bodydown in the backseat
electrical tape over his mouth
eyes feinting in this
his exaltation
his final solitude.

In the final scene, they find me—the castrated serial killer with a
deranged mind—shivering, smothered in thickmoviesugar blood,
in the fetal position on the floor of the projector room
reliving a thousand,
a billion years

of historical memory

But we're not there, yet—

The boy finds me in the darkchambers, he rips back the veils.

& I want his fist to sink my face

Batter me, lash me, dematerialize my thoughts.

Grab me by the arms and shake me. Like God

& my chest is shrapnel sludge, I can't stop its course works wrecking its way through yr fingers

Break me until I am dead dead, defibrillate me

Some ice at the center: Mythic pith Arcadia, you'll suckle, thighs locking around my hips my hand yr hand, tugging you up & down

A thousand skins

Find this knife, my sign. & Terminus

Spilling across my stomach—a mysterious face, printing the cloth.

Hyperbolic music, tensors slipped continuous, outpacing language. Lost in the penumbra, tremulous purling invading, tides extinguishing. Tendrils, tell me what to feel.

In the reddark, discrete throat, ridges dilated. Language I'm choking

The miracle split the orb in/
to kaleidoscopic fractures   the exhaled light ripples
iridescent fuguestates—

The un/dead cosmonaut is reaching his black glove across irreal space
Toward me

Chunky stars crumbledown, stabbingout in
Their wet mineral fires—

I rise up from prayercaught in the antiphon, silence. The trees hushed the night vault's sides, the wind rattling its malediction
Bad dreampoison.

I step to him, breathless rush. He takes me in his carcass body surrounding, overtaking mine

My floodsteps, earthquaking, my wild thoughts branches
Reaching with his padded palms, he stills them

His space helmet against my head.

Sapping fixtures unclenched ventricular

I start burning the worlddown
in strips

& there you are
—fuming gold

Searchpartysludge, I am the aftermath, the after image smolderedin

& you're driving toward Veracruz and the industrial fires
Disjoint colors

The smoke stacks pinnacles abounding and nothing divulged. That you were raddling in the index, yr mother spent out in the long night combustions, the mirage catalyzed.

Bending geometrical lights—

The term's insistent in yr mouth, rendering selfflowers, God's volcanoes.

Possessive re-membering elements fell—systrophes, symptomatic flames.

Scoring crossed the plain—this chronic formalism, acute. & Lightvoided

Knifingout—interregnums, a repetitive enigma predicated on. False movement lexicon

is the voice escaping

Only parentheticals

Slid abysses—graveled, yr body in fractures.

The powers of obscurity draped with mosssinking fossils. Whatever felt, given teeth

Lingering zones of autodestruction, evil engraved shrouded rituals. Could almost comprehend the kinesthetic, resonant intoxication.

The Chest exploding—climb inside this cavity with me, framed saints in iconostasis fold swooning at the threshold, wind keened.

Under an equal sign, transfigured them an essence—groan.

Truth jerking out from the pelvis, breath's rapid steps punctuated plosives.

Imperiled twisting forms veils the voice wrapped
In & in

Goblets : confused awe spills

Fibrous muscles, sinew music—

My hand finds your throat, gristly rope that bends /backpressing below the stomach, to feel the abdomen shaking, toneshifting, there.

When my tongue finds You lose yr shit—throw me onto my back, folding my legs in toward the cave my stomach defined, my bound chest—when presences ignite, dig yr teeth into my thigh.

Cataclysmic, pouringout

Air rushing through the cavity, dripping, like a bladededge.

Thunderstorms of music

Joining and parting kneeled thrashing—affronted with pleasure, stress patterned irritated ligatures—echo infinity arches yr body: monstrous contagion. Turbulence, burnt dust.

& Chemical, decay fulminating.

I was demasted, complexing glowing surrounded—

Buckled then

shineshineshine

Destroyed: a cavern, the wind nested

Defamiliarized leave it
Behind

Around the dark table, and there are silences.

That the language wound is the self-evident thought, threads depthed-fallowing.

Silenced myself at yr face, crestlines decomposed, in/to the words

Named on my knees.

Stripped yrself offshadows. Transplanting across a sparkbarrier—

Before the forever unwinds
in the thorned

Eversible destinies

—Die in the anabolic night

Syntagmatic still, irremisible thought

Gnawed.

Seeping outside lines, the seedspilled, overfull

Eardrumming secretion's urgent contingency. Circumvoluting you

Wet lacquered nacreous, the electrical path—skinned yr self shins

End branches snagged, concerning a voyeur
Pertained to this—
incomprehensiblelike
kinesthetic ritual

Intended the mind.

Still fabricating

Miscreation—called with hearing

Charred, metallic flowers strangethirsted. Heat workingthru mercury. Beaded the last word in the body /wind alveoli, without integrity.

Prosopagnosia, an interred space: grave of irises.

Derange vision—what is it the side of/fr

Gushing uncontrollable desire, I try to recombine yr body before me. Obsessive maladaptation lurching the walls, a thoughtwound kisses up devouring
You

Bad conscience, this need—drinking prisms.

Inutilizable, degradation's stint

Beautiful material eternity.

The room pressingout anguish—

&you are groundup, crystals

Phainesthai, reality shrouds he arrives at the limit trailing flame. The brain poiesis the crime that bound us. Love is cunning music, the symbolic knife.

Horrors that filled the mind crouched, in the darkvoluptuous

Here you are, stuttering & flaring.

Anchored to a wall, invisible chains intricated, tethering ghosts.

Crumpled shadows, this ineffable irremediable point you couldn't passback.

By nature, existing

&The great scales of time. Ending

I saw myself, saw myself as equal and opposed to the world

Invented, by the seeing—Gone & come back.

Aristeia wrought rhapsodic, a chord strictures honed residue, burden creased rupture-vestige.

Ecliptically extremity—raw circuitry, fissures disgorged.

Winnow time redolent, fr columns. Bonfires fuse borders bone ridges calcified

A shore transmuted longing—

Epistolary witness, incongruous, troughed whistles rot through. A medium /latitude—infernal servitude.

Space, a mourning datum. Sonic reverberant. Ghost threads shadow erosion.

Infatuation motif—my abyss in overture

The word splinters shard, gradient can you bear. Precipitate edge—

Slipping, almost grounded

Suckholes spectral. Come unalloyed. & bleeding

A net of branches mouthing lobes dark dark dark.

Ingeminate, mute witness. Turgid bed dividing you closer.

But you are alone in that morguedark, thought sickened worsening,
mi querido—febrile cords tangled.

You course like sleepthrough my arms

In the desert, salt crystals yr lips Drinking tempered violences, is this what I am
Cold Fire Finding you with my mouth, the night
Fangs

He is dancing to inaugurate the anomie of dark distance—on the dance floor Neonheld
Featureless as mist The branching forth—Extensivity

Wherephenomena, as-if appearing.
Alien emergences in Perpendicular lines They never Stop

Mechanic flux—Weeping and Seeping through the floor the bodies Shimmer

Hungdown

Flexing moon Worlds The palaces of a diamond In Furnaced

Grids expound denotative Harmonies Accorded octave you strum
Its alveole Inside

You

Are not yours. Drink from my eyes
::Telekinetic wind

Mutter smut in the desert saltlands Death materialized, Ravaging
the face

Blood on the linoleum Gone trailing—the Violent hands of Clouds

The self identical That You were, when touching Combustion

Blood knots, The bodysap condensing—Incredible Alterity Forging
the fingers Throb through
Machines

—Dead surrounds Permutating before: An open palm

Expiating a violence You don't understand, yet

It dominates forms Salt haunted Earth fringes The Chain react
Surfaces

Undressed first–Skin petals of Boyhood

You grind—Guzzling Poison

Psychagogy

Mulchclutter, Yr ballasted in My arms Streetlights blast it down continuous Truthhead

I need to feel you swarming around me—

The highway dominion. Veins circulating Contagions

Pressing into a top, a mirror Ricocheted
back, &—

Immerse yourself In the stillwater

Andcomeback
And die
And die
And die
And comeback
And die

What burned through expression

Soft Ore

Dick sliding in rough resistances

I hallucinate yr body kneeling over me. White flashing—persisting in its fire, licking the night insides

Reminded the self of self, in prohibition, language as anamnesiac had reference only to the words-itself—fell undecidable, inside the mind.

And I am trying to write out the burning interstices. Within it

Until so conditioned to expect suffering,
Enter into language.

Came disentangled from the world I thought
mine.

On the way to inexistence—metalanguage

No propositions or syntax, we are blendable flows, come toward me.

Streaming voices, yr aural secretions briefly intermingled, then becoming extinct. The enunciation is alien. The image is dissipative—tending to dissolve everything around, with it.

Rather than being seen, melt. The recorded voice, taut silence. Just spatially determined—

Equidistant vertices, inexorable. Ordered disorder, consubstantial with yr body.

The only thing I know how to do is to come-disentangled from a net, and run dredgewailing thru the streets, covered in my family's blood, metaphor—borne thru a tunnel. Burning through a truss—dehisce beneath my hands. Decomposing themes, centrally—erode.

Ghostly dimensions, punctuating the silences, lie on the ground defunctionalized. Devitalizing Mind—just noise, never wanders.

The underknives, a specimen, yr heart called in in fragmentations. Billows were roiling and smolder, drinking to insert voids into the composition, blanksout

Where you were swimming down— exhausting language, the sea that swallows-obscure corridors.

Don't you ever tremolo?

Ghostly sentinel in the ice age, unable to rise, because of the memorial weapon's voice, like a limit to infinity. Pure lines of abolition, from void to void, I thought I almost saw the figure, uncontoured.

Never separate from its disappearance—only described through its descent.

I thrust aside the wall, that before I had crumbledthrough, rippedup delved, droppedin. In the form of a deer now, abandoning the body, shaking off the icelacquered antlers, the human inset. I don't even move.

I press aside the wall. Because the space was never there. To erect an image erect wrecks inside, where do yr strings end?

Words drove circuits underground, bedrock blasted—and arrive undone, the events blurs. The spirits forged, behind our backs, as lungs withered. The image is only hands, touching yr mind,
let the glowing waves fondle the metallic cavity, where yr dreams fermented and tortuously, return

"A court of law is a highly homosexual libidinal site"

"Some of us are part of Nature, and some not."

"The term 'unnatural', used by the police in the nineteenth century to describe homosexuals, finds its true definition: it describes the person who is against nature as the guarantor both of desire and of its repression."

Preceded by a negative sign, persecution mythos. What delimited you, an inconsolable excess.

He keeps a case file on his own perversions, wrapping and unwrapping the desire objects/subjects—Beneath the emergency lights, a rationalized human law: protective rigid expedient against crimes—against Nature.

Told you to find a masochist in yr heart, do you believe in perfectibility

Desire that overspills the social codes—Yr idiolect, irresistible, uncapturable.

The legislation of the self undergone, driving it down, and mitigated.

What you are You are You Are

Hard grain, background strobing streetlight, pastureland let me glean you yours, differentiating without control

Radio static burbling
—In the cabin

The law in yr thought circumscribing modes of expression, unbind them Its edge and end–incising you. Yr recollective errors, historico-hallucinatory—Render yrself unnamable

Cryovolcanic Man
Locked-in stone

Statuary Sentinel.

Bronze gates, the mist flung scintillating

The soft lock of yr mouth
Dust vessel, I feel you
—A blue electrical storm ball

Mnemonic patina. Pillars swollen—into the night. Tone plucking tone, you drizzle, husking scales. The gaze looses, earth hollows its vowel. Turn /sole. In violet clumps. &meadows yielding

"I feel beautiful and holy with my missing cock"

Pith conflagrate, runny fingers The song stripped Can't Rememory. Yrs? Lips, scum blossoms. Bloodthirsts—

Mouthlike orthographic noise, Yr judicious fealty

Calyx, I stud there. Weave yr hair plaintive. Enwreathed plaits—
Voicesmelting

And I can hear everything that you are

And I will be rapidly eroded by natural forces

And you are reorganizing yourself around the absence at the center of you, when he pullsout, leaking, wanting to be

A field of freedom beneath you.

Trample hoof/beats

But that's impossible—

Finding yr self there Violence

Dry breath in the night
Scraping the flung branches

The Colossus

The Aegean waves turmoiled, pellucid in their pull. And crashing—as a massive cosmonautical figure rose from the sea. In two lumbering steps, that set the world to seism, he took the Greek island in a wide-legged straddle, its volcanic crater. A watery visionless eyeball. Recording, recording… His massive thighs, calves disappearing into the surf, the body stood unnamed.

And so.

You have to leave now, she says

I am with my mother's body